The Devil's Pool

The Devil's Pool

George Sand

Translated by Andrew Brown

ET REMOTISSIMA PROPE

Hesperus Classics

Hesperus Classics
Published by Hesperus Press Limited
4 Rickett Street, London sw6 1ru
www.hesperuspress.com

First published in French as *La Mare au Diable* in 1846
This translation first published by Hesperus Press Limited, 2005

Introduction and English language translation © Andrew Brown, 2005
Foreword © Victoria Glendinning, 2005

Designed and typeset by Fraser Muggeridge
Printed in Italy by Graphic Studio Srl

ISBN: 1-84391-105-1

CONTENTS

Reading this book takes me back to a stuffy little book room in my convent boarding school. I was sixteen, the same age as 'little Marie' in the story. A small group of us who were good at French had special classes with Mademoiselle Fénice – no grammar, no translation, no conversation, just reading books and stories in French. We all, including Mademoiselle, took turns to read aloud. I retained from that long-ago time not the story of *La Mare au Diable* (its title in French), but the bewitched atmosphere – the ride through the countryside, the darkness coming down, the swirling mist, the horse rearing up and bolting, and the scariness of the forest at night. This is the stuff of fairy stories, and *The Devil's Pool* has always been thought suitable for young people because it is short, simple, and has no explicitly rude bits in it. Reading it now, I see that it is not so simple, and that there is a great deal in it about the sexual imperative – both the violent, dark, 'devil's pool' of lust (controlled, just, by Germain, but not by Marie's employer) and the burning desire which, when mutual, leads to marriage and children. Marriage is shown as a crucial 'glue' in the functioning of the community.

Little Marie is curiously complicated. It is acknowledged that she is of an age to be married, yet she calls herself a child and is treated as one by Germain, who is twenty-eight. In the French he calls her '*tu*' and she calls him, respectfully, '*vous*'. She is docile, dutiful, and self-denying beyond belief, and yet obviously brighter and quicker that Germain, who apparently cannot do the farm accounts. It is she who saves up food, lights a fire in a damp wood, improvises a bed for the little boy, roasts chestnuts and plucks birds with incredible speed. Obviously she is no fool. So, is her apparent obliviousness to Germain's sexual attraction to her genuine? Is she only pretending not to know what he longs for when he lays his head on her breast beside the head of his little son, or when he bends over her as if to kiss her, waking her from sleep, or when she snuggles close to him under his cloak on the road? Such transparent innocence in a sixteen year old is unusual to say the least, but I think George Sand wants us to believe in it. She is, after all, 'little Marie', described, in her wedding dress, as not yet fully developed: her 'petite figure' would 'inevitably grow and fill out'.

It is more understandable that she is 'astonished' when Germain first proposes, telling him that she thinks of him as 'an uncle or a godfather' and, even more candidly, that all her friends would laugh at her if she married someone so old – a very teenage reaction. Her other objection, culled from her mother's lore – that she would not want to be lumbered in her middle age with an old husband who could not work – shows, in contrast, a mature peasant realism. Anyway, she did not love him: 'I just don't have those feelings for you in my heart.' But at what point, then, did she begin to love him? This is not clear.

I was interested to read in George Sand's own Introduction – the second one, five years after the book was first published – that her aim was to write something 'very touching and simple, and that I did not bring it off quite as I wanted'. Maybe that was because she did not let the story speak for itself. There is quite a lot of George Sand in it. She cannot just let Marie and Germain show what they are like through their speech and actions. She spells out, in advance, the unselfconscious quality of the peasant mind; Germain does not see the beauties of nature as the artist would, though he is at one with the soil he ploughs – and with the beasts who pull the plough too, for the oxen and horses show their own capacity for affection and for sorrow. The ox who loses his companion (as Germain lost his first wife) mourns and sickens. Old Grey, the mother of Germain's mare, is distressed to see Young Grey cantering out of the village (just as little Marie and her mother wept on parting). Germain would not thrive away from what he knows. A nearby village is almost like a foreign country. He is childlike, unevolved.

To an extent, Sand is writing a fable or parable, to convey the essential goodness and fulfilment that can illuminate such apparently narrow lives, in contrast to the 'fake enlightenment' of her sophisticated readers. Though she does underline the ugly side of customs such as the arranged marriage, with its potential for exploitation and humiliation, she deliberately highlights the poetic and pure side of rural life, as opposed to squalor and suffering. Early deaths and endemic poverty are treated here as part of natural life; and natural life, with its indomitable, instinctive force for continuity, is what she is celebrating.

There is a powerful undercurrent of regret for the disappearance of age-old country customs in her native region; what we would now call the social anthropologist in her is well to the fore in the account of traditional marriage games, tacked on as a coda. She wants rural life to go on in the old predestined way, but with some better understanding of the value of that life.

These seem conservative, even sentimental attitudes for a liberated free-thinking, free-loving, progressive woman like Sand. But the story must also be read, as she intended, as an act of empathy with her characters, and a riposte to intellectual arrogance. In any case, we all perversely love what we have chosen to lose – in her case, the simple life. The story was written, originally for magazine publication, at top speed. The unresolved ambivalences and contradictions make *The Devil's Pool*, as its author knew, an imperfect work of art. It is all the more intriguing for being so. For all its simple charm, it seems to me a book for grown-ups, and worth reading more than once.

– Victoria Glendinning, 2005

Charles Baudelaire speculated that George Sand was 'possessed' (by the Devil): her apparent 'kindly heart' and 'common sense' were a façade for something much darker. This is not the place to rehearse Baudelaire's idiosyncratic judgements (which say more about him than about Sand), but maybe *The Devil's Pool* is in fact less innocent than it at first seems. On the surface, the tale seems straightforward enough: it was dashed off by Sand in a mere four days, has been cherished as a children's story for generations, and is imbued with the understated, Corot-like lyricism of Sand's native region of the Berry, with its gently undulating heaths, its slow rivers and tranquil marshlands. A certain limpidity is indeed an important aspect of the book's charm, but it is still haunted by the devil present in its title, and the pool over which he apparently presides is the centre of the story's moral and narrative geography: it is by this pool's treacherous waters that the ploughman Germain, his young son Petit-Pierre, and the sixteen-year-old Marie find themselves obliged to spend a foggy night when they get lost in the woods on their way to the village of Fourche. Their attempts to find the path from which they have wandered echo, faintly but insistently, the 'dark wood' in which Dante finds himself lost at the beginning of the *Divine Comedy*, and like him they at first find themselves going round in circles (though, as for Dante, this sojourn among the tangled trees eventually turns out to have been the prelude to a great good). Germain's horse bolts (a bolting horse in a forest is a staple ingredient of horror stories), while Petit-Pierre is worried about wolves coming to gobble him up – a nice fairy-tale touch, we might think, were it not for the fact that wolves were still a very real menace in the forests of the Berry as late as the 1870s. Later on, a panic-stricken Germain, convinced that something terrible has happened to the young people in his care during their stay in Fourche, gallops back into the forest only to find an old woman (a crone? a witch?) gathering wood there. She is the one who tells him that the place he had spent the night is called the Devil's Pool; it's a bad spot and unless you perform the right spell you risk encountering misfortune, and – as Germain has just discovered – anyone who stops there at night-time will be obliged to wait until dawn before being able to leave. When Germain anxiously asks after the children, she replies that a little boy has been drowned in the pool… (Sand herself, as a young woman, was suicidally drawn to the allure of ponds and rivers.) In short, nature is far from the cosy, homely place you might have expected: it is threatening and uncanny. Petit-Pierre's dead mother speaks to him there, and a cross put up in commemoration of an earlier victim of the pool was thrown into its waters, one stormy night, by evil spirits.

Nor is the story socially 'innocent' either. Some of Sand's critics have thought she patronised the peasants she wrote about, but Sand herself was alert to the risk of idealisation – so alert, in fact, that she drew attention to it in not just one preface but two, arguing simultaneously (and rather defensively) *both* that she was not really writing a realistic novel but an idyll, a pastoral, as escapist in its way as the bucolic fantasies of the courtly culture of earlier ages, *and* that her work was perfectly realistic in that she had shown virtuous peasants (and they *did* exist – or at least, they *could*) while so many other writers had concentrated one-sidedly on the tedium, toil, ignorance and squalor of peasant life. It is true that the picture of rural existence drawn by other nineteenth-century French writers was generally negative: from Balzac's *The Peasants* (unfinished, but serialised in 1844) to Zola's *The Earth* (1887), and from Stendhal's far-from-idyllic depiction of life in the Jura Mountains in *The Red and the Black* (1830) to Maupassant's 1880s Normandy tales, the peasantry was represented as brutalised, rapacious and doltish (or, at best, endowed with a sly cunning). These works suggest why Marx (who had little direct experience of it) might have referred scathingly to the 'idiocy of rural life'. In contrast to these disenchanted accounts, *The Devil's Pool* and its successors (*Little Fadette* (1848), *François the Foundling* (also 1848) and *The Master Pipers* (1853)) extol the provincial, the rural and the earthy, and apparently deplore the corruptions of city life, the inroads of technology and the loss of peasant traditions. But rural life is far from being sweet and innocent in Sand's books: there is folk-dancing there, but incest too (notably in *François*). Even in *The Devil's Pool* – perhaps the most demure of her peasant fictions, the rustic charm and freshness of whose three central characters might at times have verged on the insipid – there are ripples in the water that betoken darker undercurrents. Marie may be a sixteen year old, but the text treats her in contradictory ways – frequently (especially in her speech) as a mature adult, one who seems more worldly-wise and grown-up than Germain, but also, insistently, as a child (she is persistently called 'little Marie' in contexts that deliberately work to infantilise her). That Germain, already a widower at twenty-eight-but-pushing-thirty, can fall in love with her and seek to marry her, arouses resistance on her part simply because she fancies someone younger, but there is no social condemnation. An age difference between spouses that was acceptable in a peasant community of the 1840s is barely so now, and comes (no doubt anachronistically) with a whiff of the love that, these days, dare not speak its name. True, this novel, in its 'chasteness' – remarked on by many earlier critics – is far from characteristic of Sand's œuvre as a whole (other works tackle homosexuality, incest and the transgression of gender roles with, for the time, great openness); and yet the scene in the forest at night where Germain longs to hold 'little Marie' is immensely erotic. Marie is lusted after by others, too – the farmer for whom she is going to work in Fourche, for instance, who tries to force his attentions on her the minute he sees her (behaviour which causes a weary raising of eyebrows but no real remonstration on the part of his fellow-villagers). If Marie had been a couple of years younger, the farmer from Les Ormeaux could have played Quilty to Germain's Humbert Humbert (and when Marie teasingly calls the latter an 'ogre', because of his appetite, a modern reader might momentarily be reminded of the ogres in Michel Tournier's *The Erl-King*, who prey on children in more terrifying ways). Still, the eros in Sand's novel, though intense, is too diffuse to be tied down to Germain's desire for Marie, a desire which in any case has an elemental aspect to it, being partly a protective response to the sinister outlandishness of the night-time mist-swathed forest. The birth of his love is attended and fostered by fire and water, and more than a hint of the supernatural: perhaps the real object of the more general desire that runs through the book is not so much a person as a way of life, a set of values, a landscape. And Marie is not merely contradictory as a child-woman, she is magical.

Again, though Sand's peasants here are far less rapacious than in Balzac or Zola, they are still capable of vice: the two main villages in *The Devil's Pool* almost comprise polar opposites, with Fourche being more 'bourgeois' than Belair, and thus more corrupt. Germain's intended bride-to-be, who lives in Fourche, is vain and affected, and also, like Germain, has lost a spouse though still only in her thirties; it's no wonder that Sand places Hans Holbein's *Dance of Death* as an emblematic frontispiece to her story – as mortality rates show, nature in the nineteenth century was not just *das Immergleiche*, the comforting, never-changing, ahistorical refuge of bourgeois fantasy, but a realm of alarming and deadly unpredictabilities that could at times be just as resistant to the vanity of human wishes as the harshest urban environment. Germain acts as the Düreresque Knight, keeping Death and the Devil away from those in his care.

The novel as a genre tends to be the product of a mercantile, rationalistic, urban culture (which is why novels set exclusively in the countryside are sometimes seen as vaguely deviant – 'regional', i.e. set apart from the life of capitals and thus, perhaps, a challenge to mentalities formed by capitalism). *The Devil's Pool*, with its relative absence of plot or plotting (even if its narrative does end in a particularly time-honoured fashion), and its evocations of the *longue durée* underlying the vicissitudes of peasant life, seems more like a novella (or a German *Novelle*, with its mysterious turning points, and its mixture of realism and symbolism) than a novel. It is also a work of ethnography – and like all ethnography, it is marked by an anxiety about the relation between the reporter and the human beings on whose habits and traditions he or she is reporting: is the ethnographer an observer, or a participant? The Appendix that Sand included at the request of her publisher, who thought the book was a bit short otherwise, details the wedding customs of the Berry region, customs that were already starting to fade away. In it, the authorial persona, who claimed to have gleaned Germain's story from his own lips, hovers rather uncertainly as an invisible wedding guest. This unease in narrative point of view is a mark of alienation, and reflects Sand's own ambivalent standpoint. She was born and brought up in the Berry, and mixed freely with the peasant children there, only to be sent off to a Paris convent and weaned off *Berrichon* patois. Much of her subsequent existence was utterly different from that of the peasants whose life she, as she puts it herself, 'sings' in *The Devil's Pool* (where *Berrichon* words and turns of phrase are few and far between, and graze the text in delicate italics that barely disturb the almost classical purity of the speech of Germain or Marie). Far from being a stay-at-home rustic, rooted in the slow rhythms of the French provinces, Sand travelled across Europe, was tumultuously involved in contemporary politics (she was Minister of Propaganda in the short-lived Second Republic of 1848), and contributed passionately to the debates of her age, not least on the status of women: a deracinated, cosmopolitan intellectual. In that revolutionary year 1848, she founded a newspaper; it lasted only three issues, but its title, *La Cause du Peuple* [*The People's Cause*] was the same as that of the incendiary Maoist journal that, banned by the Government, would be sold in the streets by Sartre and Beauvoir a century later. Indeed, Sand's behaviour struck many of her contemporaries not just as politically subversive, but as shocking and bizarre – as *unnatural* as that of the Baudelaire who 'accused' her of being nature incarnate. When he dyed his hair green (in homage to absinthe), he was being a naughty little boy (and was teased for it: 'everyone dyes their hair green these days,' he was told; 'now, if you'd dyed it *blue*…'); when Sand smoked cigars, wore trousers, quite openly took lovers and (worst of all) wrote novels, she was not only being eccentric (though she was just as much the dandy as, in his more desperate way, Baudelaire – though we mustn't forget that he was actually put on trial for the most significant product of his eccentricity, *The Flowers of Evil*): she was making a ground-breaking statement that flew in the face of current opinion on the things a woman could or could not do. (It is true that her retirement to the Berry after the collapse of the Republic in 1851 marks a certain retreat, but *The Devil's Pool* was written in 1846, before any such disillusionment with Paris, politics and history had become necessary. In any case, why should the countryside be seen as outside history?)

So *The Devil's Pool* is a view of peasant life from the perspective of an insider/outsider: a sophisticate's evocation of a certain simplicity. And this required more artistry than may at first meet the eye. Again, this artistry was often denied. Sand, whose *Devil's Pool* is in some ways (compared with her other novels) an experiment in minimalism, was more usually perceived as a figure of excess (too much tobacco, too many lovers, and, worst of all, *too many books* – a trifle unfair, given the immense constraints that she had to overcome in order to write just one). Her productivity itself was held against her: she just turned on a tap, and out it poured. 'She has the famous *flowing style*, so dear to the bourgeois,' said Baudelaire. And for Nietzsche she was one of '*my impossibles*', 'the milch-cow with the flowing style'. She must have touched a raw nerve to make such intelligent men say such stupid things. ('Yes, yes, Herr Professor Nietzsche, very witty, very droll, "a milch-cow", I *quite* see your point: *lactea ubertas* and all that. Now, about this Superman…') There is, inevitably, an ideological point at stake. It seems that the 'flowing style' (an imprecise term, but one that does express the sense of liquidity and transparency that the reader may find in *The Devil's Pool*) is the polar opposite of the drier, more 'atomistic' ways of depicting reality that we find in Baudelaire or in Sand's devoted friend and admirer Flaubert, who in their very different ways adhered largely, and with many qualifications, to an aesthetic predicated on discontinuity, interruption, fragmentation and irony (as well as costiveness of production and 'perfection' of form) rather than smoothness, holism, empathy and flow. Historically, the gritted teeth and aesthetic aloofness of Baudelaire and Flaubert tended to triumph over the effusions, the strangely osmotic characterisation, and the apparent 'sincerity' of Sand. The conflict between these two ways of seeing echoes through later cultural history: it finds an avatar in the opposition between the parched and particular perceptions of Leopold Bloom, all bitty and alert and darting, and the maundering meandering flow of Molly's stream of consciousness. This can lead to some fateful polarisations: sometimes Sand, with her 'flowing style' and love of humanity, is pressed into service as standing for Life with a capital L, over Flaubert's paralysed panic in the face of the said commodity and his distaste for mankind's enormous *bêtise*. Maybe – though a single laconic sentence in the 'misanthropic' Flaubert might occasionally be ten times more imbued with real life and humanity than any amount of vaguely humanitarian *bavardage*. But then, there is so much more to Sand than that.

Finally, the apparent artlessness of the story is also made more complex by what follows it – the Appendix. As with the short treatise on gypsy life that Mérimée added to *Carmen*, Sand's ethnographic essay tacked on at the end of her tale is not just a space-filling supplement, but of real interest in itself. Here the sheer otherness of country life, even to those who live in it – nature's mysteries, its powers of reproduction and regeneration as well as destruction – is brought out with great force. Perhaps *this* was the crux of Baudelaire's grouse against Sand: that for all the bondieuserie we find in works such as *The Devil's Pool*, which ends with Germain's morning prayer, there is something deeply pagan in her work (found more explicitly in such Spinozistic-pantheistic speculations as her earlier novel *Spiridion*). The Berry is, together with Brittany, one of the two French regions where pagan superstition (or powerfully persistent ideas about the relations between human beings and the cosmos) have tended to flourish most tenaciously. A priest from the church of Notre-Dame de Bourges, on the edge of Sand's *terroir* (what could have been called, if the author's name were pronounced as its English equivalent, 'Sandland') told a friend of mine that the Catholic Church had more or less given up on the Berry, with its witches and its pagan superstitions and its dark magic. 'We sent our missionaries elsewhere – to Africa and Asia, where people understood them better,' he sighed. Not even two thousand years of Christianity managed to oust the spirits and replace them with Spirit. Sand's Appendix to *The Devil's Pool* is filled with the cries of lamenting cranes, heading across dark skies like lost souls seeking rest; nature is Mahler's Sixth Symphony, with its forebodings and its bereft shrieks and lamentations, as well as Beethoven's. And she shows how innocent japes with a cabbage seem to echo the rites of Priapus that doubtless date back, in one guise or another, thousands of years. Have we entirely overcome such fascinations? On one level (that of the longest *durée*), perhaps we are all still pagans ('country bumpkins', as the term originally meant). Perhaps, for better or worse, Europe was only ever half Christianised (it is significant that the wedding at the end of *The Devil's Pool* takes place some way away from the village, as if the parish were a somewhat marginal element in the peasants' lives)… Be that as it may, it is at least clearer why Sand's story is not just an escapist fantasy, nor an idyll, nor an innocent love story, nor even simply a regional tone poem: it is literature itself, that devil's pool in which we see our own fears and longings, and from which it is so difficult to escape.

– *Andrew Brown, 2005*

Note on the Text:
I have used the text of *La Mare au Diable* (Paris: Nelson, 1945), but I have also consulted the edition by Léon Cellier (Paris: Gallimard Folio Classique, 1999).

It is to my friend Hugo Azérad that I owe the story of the Berrichon priest – and so much else besides. This translation is for him, with esteem and affection.

The Devil's Pool

PREFACE

When, with *The Devil's Pool*, I embarked on a series of rural novels that I intended to collect together under the title of *The Hemp Crusher's Evenings*, it was not with any systematic purpose, or any claim to be revolutionising literature. Nobody can carry out a revolution single-handed, and there are revolutions – especially in the arts – that humanity brings about without really knowing how, because everyone plays a part in the process. But this is not applicable to the novel of rustic manners: it has always existed, in every shape and size, sometimes pompous, sometimes mannered, sometimes naive. As I have said, and will say here again, the dream of rural life has always been the ideal of towns and cities and even of royal courts. I have done nothing new by following the inclination that leads civilised men back to the charms of primitive life. I have sought neither to create a new language, nor to develop a new manner for myself. And yet this is just what has been asserted in a fair number of reviews. But I know my own intentions better than anyone, and I'm always astonished that criticism makes such a fuss and to-do when the simplest idea, the most humdrum circumstance, are the only inspirations to which artistic productions owe their being. For *The Devil's Pool* in particular, it was merely the fact which I mention in my introduction – seeing an engraving by Holbein that particularly struck me, and a real scene that was in front of my eyes at the same time, during the sowing season – that had impelled me to write this modest tale, set amidst the humble landscapes through which I would wander each day. If anyone asks me what my aim was, I will reply that I wanted to write something very touching and simple, and that I did not bring it off quite as I wanted. Yes, I saw and sensed the beauty in simplicity – but to see and to depict are two entirely different things! The best the artist can hope for is to persuade those with eyes to take a look for themselves. So, Readers, see the simplicity, see the sky and the fields, and the trees, and the peasants, especially what is good and true about them: you will see them to some extent in my book, but you will see them much better in nature.

– *George Sand*
Nohant, 12th April 1851

The Author to the Reader

In the sweat of your brow
You live your poor life:
Long trouble and strife,
Then Death comes for you.

The quatrain in Old French, written under a composition by Holbein, is, in its naivety, profoundly sad. The engraving shows a ploughman driving his plough across the middle of a field. The vast countryside stretches out into the distance, with poor shacks dotted here and there; the sun is setting behind the hill. It is the end of a day of hard labour. The peasant is an old, tough man, covered in rags. The team of four horses that he is driving before him is skinny and exhausted; the ploughshare digs into rough and recalcitrant terrain. There is only one creature who is light-hearted and sprightly in this scene of *trouble and strife*. It is a fantastical personage, a skeleton armed with a whip, running in the furrow alongside the frightened horses and belabouring them, thus serving as a ploughboy to the old farmer. It is Death, the spectre that Holbein allegorically introduced into the succession of philosophical and religious subjects, at once gloomy and farcical, entitled *The Simulacra of Death*[1].

In this collection, or rather in this vast composition in which Death, playing his role on every page, acts as the common thread and the dominant idea, Holbein displayed them all: sovereigns, pontiffs, lovers, gamblers, drunkards, nuns, courtesans, brigands, the poor, warriors, monks, Jews, travellers – all the characters of his time and ours; and everywhere the spectre of Death, mocking, menacing and triumphant. From only one picture is Death absent. This is the one where poor Lazarus, lying on a dunghill at the rich man's door, declares that he does not fear death, doubtless because he has nothing to lose and his whole life is an anticipation of death.

Is this stoic idea, from the semi-pagan Christianity of the Renaissance, really consoling, and are religious souls satisfied by it?

The ambitious man, the deceitful man, the tyrant, the lecher – those haughty sinners who misuse their lives and whom Death drags away by their hair – they are all going to be punished, no doubt. But are the blind man, the beggar, the madman and the poor peasant compensated for their prolonged wretchedness by the mere reflection that death is not a misfortune for them? No! An implacable sadness, a terrible sense of doom hangs heavy over the artist's work. It is like a bitter curse hurled at the fate of humanity.

And here, indeed, resides the painful satire, and the authentic depiction of the society that Holbein could see all around him. Crime and wretchedness, these are the things that struck him; but what about us, artists of another century – what will *we* depict? Will we seek in the idea of death the remuneration of present-day mankind? Will we call on it as the punishment of injustice and the recompense for suffering?

No, our business is no longer with death, but with life. We no longer believe either in the nothingness of the tomb, nor in a salvation purchased by a forced renunciation; we want life to be good, because we want it to be fruitful. Lazarus must leave his dunghill so that a poor man will no longer rejoice at the rich man's death. Everyone must be happy so that the happiness of a few will not be criminal and cursed by God. The ploughman, as he sows his wheat, must know that his labours are a way of working for life, and not rejoice at the idea that Death is walking at his side. Finally, death must no longer be a punishment for prosperity, nor a consolation for distress. God created death neither to punish nor to recompense people for life; he blessed life, and the tomb must not be a refuge to which we can send those whom we are unwilling to make happy.

Certain artists of our time, taking a long hard look at their surroundings, devote themselves to depicting the pain, the abjection and the poverty – Lazarus' dunghill. This may lie within the domain of art and philosophy, but is their aim achieved by the way they depict poverty as so ugly, so debased, sometimes so immoral and so criminal? And is the effect of their depiction actually salutary in the way they would wish it to be? I would not presume to pronounce a verdict on this matter. People may point out that, by showing this abyss dug beneath the fragile soil of opulence, these artists are striking terror into the heart of the wicked rich man, just as, in the age of the *danse macabre*, they showed him his grave wide open to receive him, and Death ready to enfold him in the embrace of its foul arms. Today, the rich man is shown the burglar picking the lock on his door and the ever-watchful murderer waiting for him to doze off. I must confess that I am not entirely sure how the rich man is to be reconciled with the human beings he despises, or how he will be brought to sympathise with the sufferings of the poor man whom he fears, by being shown the poor man as an escaped jailbird and a night prowler. Dreadful Death, grinding his teeth and playing the violin in the images of Holbein and his predecessors, did not manage, in this guise, to convert the perverse and console the victims. Might our literature be proceeding, in this respect, rather like the artists of the Middle Ages and the Renaissance?

Holbein's drinkers fill their goblets with a sort of furious zest to ward off the idea of Death which, entirely invisible to them, acts as their cupbearer. Today's wicked rich men demand fortifications and cannons to ward off the idea of a peasant uprising[2], which art shows being busily prepared in the shadows, in every detail, waiting for the moment to strike at the current state of society. The medieval Church responded to the terrors of the powerful of the earth by the sale of indulgences. Today's government assuages the anxieties of the rich by getting them to cough up the money for a great number of gendarmes and jailers, bayonets and prisons.

Albrecht Dürer, Michelangelo, Holbein, Callot and Goya all produced powerful satires on the ills of their age and their countries.[3] These are immortal works, historic pages of unquestionable value; so we do not wish to deny to artists the right to probe the wounds of society and lay them bare before our eyes, but isn't there something else that needs to be done now, something other than the depiction of terror and menace? In this literature of dark and sinister mysteries made fashionable by talent and imagination, I prefer the mild and gentle figures to the dramatic villains. The former may aim successfully at bringing about changes of heart, but the latter spread fear, and fear does not cure egotism but increases it.

It is my belief that the mission of Art is a mission based on the emotions and on love, and that the novel today should replace the parables and apologias of naive periods of history; the artist has a broader and more poetic task than that of proposing a few measures of caution and reconciliation that will damp down the panic inspired by his depictions. His aim ought to be that of inducing people to love the objects of his care, and at a pinch I would not criticise him were he to embellish them a little. Art is not a study of positive reality; it is a quest for ideal reality, and *The Vicar of Wakefield* was a more useful book, and more wholesome for the soul, than *The Perverted Peasant* and *Dangerous Liaisons*.[4]

Reader, forgive me for these reflections, and be so kind as to accept them as a kind of preface. There won't be any such reflections in the little story I am going to tell you, and it will be so short and simple that I needed to apologise in advance, and tell you what I think about horror stories.

It was a ploughman who made me veer off and embark on this digression. And it was indeed the story of a ploughman that I intended to tell you, and that I am now going to relate.

2
Ploughing

I had just been gazing at length, with a profound sense of melancholy, at Holbein's ploughman, and I was walking through the countryside, dreaming of the life of the fields and the destiny of the farmer. It's doubtless a gloomy prospect – having to wear out your strength and the days of your life splitting open the womb of the possessive earth, who will not relinquish the treasures of her fecundity without a struggle, when a hunk of the blackest and coarsest bread at the end of the day is the only recompense and the sole profit to be gained from such harsh labour. Those riches that cover the soil, those harvests, those fruits, those proud beasts growing fat on the long grass, are the property of a few, and instruments which exhaust and enslave the greatest number. The man of leisure generally loves for their own sake, not the fields, nor the meadows, nor the spectacle of nature, nor the superb animals that are to be converted into gold coins for his use. The man of leisure comes looking for a bit of fresh air and health during his stay in the country; then he returns to the cities where he will spend the fruit of his vassals' labour.

For his part, the labouring man is too overburdened, too wretched and too apprehensive about the future to enjoy the beauty of the countryside and the charms of rustic life. For him, too, the golden fields, the lovely meadows and the superb animals represent bags of gold crowns – of which he will get only a small proportion, inadequate for his needs – and yet these cursed bags need to be filled by the labourer, year after year, to satisfy his master and pay for the right to live, pinching and scraping a wretched existence, on his land.

And yet, Nature is eternally young, beautiful and generous. She showers poetry and beauty onto every creature, and onto every plant, so that they are able to grow and flourish to their fullest extent. She possesses the secret of happiness, and no one has been able to wrest it from her. The happiest of men would be he who, in possession of the skill of cultivation, and working with his own hands, drawing well-being and liberty from the exercise of his intelligent strength, would have enough time to live by his heart and his brain to understand his own work and to love that of God. The artist has intense pleasures of this kind, in the contemplation and reproduction of the beauties of nature; but at the sight of the sorrows of the men who populate this paradise on earth, the artist whose heart is upright and humane is troubled in the midst of his enjoyment. Happiness would be where the mind, the heart and the arms worked in concert under the eye of Providence, and a holy harmony prevailed between the munificence of God and the ecstasies of the human soul. Then, instead of the pitiful and dreadful figure of Death, striding down his furrow, whip in hand, the painter of allegories could place at his side a radiant angel, sowing great handfuls of the blessed grain onto the steaming furrow.

And the dream of a mild, free, poetic, laborious and simple life for the man of the fields is not so very difficult to conceive and need not be relegated to the realm of pure fantasy. Virgil's sweet and melancholy words, 'Oh happy the man of the fields, if only he could be aware of his happiness!'[5] express a certain nostalgia, but like all nostalgia, they are also a prediction. A day will come when the ploughman, too, will be an artist, if not able to express (and in any case such a thing will not really be so important then), at least to *feel* beauty. Does anyone think that this mysterious intuition of poetry is not already present within him, as an instinct and a vague daydream? Among those who are protected by a certain comfort, and among whom excessive wretchedness has not stifled all moral and intellectual development, happiness – pure, felt and appreciated – is found in a rudimentary state; and in any case, if poets' voices have risen from the midst of sorrow and weariness, who is to say that manual labour excludes the functions of the soul? Doubtless this exclusion is the general result of excessive labour and profound poverty, but let no one say that when man works moderately and usefully there will be none but bad workmen and bad poets. He who draws noble pleasures from the feeling for poetry is a true poet, even if he has never written a line of poetry in his entire life.

My thoughts had been following this train of ideas, and I had not realised that this confidence in man's educability was being fortified within me by external influences. I was walking along the edge of a field that the peasants were busy preparing for the forthcoming sowing. The arena was as vast as that in Holbein's picture. The landscape, too, was vast, and its broad swathes of verdure, starting to go red here and there at the approaches of autumn, framed this extensive terrain, a vigorous brown in hue, where recent rain had left, in some of the furrows, streaks of water gleaming in the sunshine like slender silver threads. The day was clear and warm, and the earth, freshly opened by the sharp ploughshares, was breathing out a light vapour. At the top of the field, an old man, whose broad back and stern face resembled that in Holbein, but whose clothes did not suggest poverty, was gravely driving his old-fashioned *plough*, drawn by two tranquil oxen with pale yellow coats, veritable patriarchs of the meadow, tall of stature, a little skinny, with long, turned-down horns – old workers who have, by long habit, been transformed into *brothers*, as they are called in our countryside, and who, if deprived of one another, refuse to work with a new companion and let themselves die of sorrow. People unfamiliar with the countryside view the friendship shown by the ox for the fellow-ox who helps him pull the plough as a fable. They should come and see, at the far end of the cowshed, the poor skinny and exhausted animal, flicking its emaciated sides with its anxious tail, snorting fearfully and disdainfully at the food presented to it, its eyes continually turned to the door, pawing the empty place next to it, sniffing the yokes and the chains that its companion had borne, and ceaselessly calling out for its partner with heart-breaking bellows. The oxherd will say, 'There's a spoilt ox-team; his brother has died, and this one won't ever work again. We ought to be able to fatten him up for the slaughter, but he won't eat, and before very long he'll be dead of starvation.'

The old ploughman was working slowly, silently, without any useless exertions. His docile team was in no more of a hurry than he was, but thanks to the continuity of undistracted labour, and an expenditure of skilled and sustained force, his furrow was dug as quickly as his son's, who, some distance away, was driving four less robust oxen, along a vein of more resistant and stony land.

But what drew my attention just then really was a fine spectacle, a noble subject for a painter. At the other end of the arable field, a hale and hearty young man was driving a magnificent team: four pairs of young animals, their dark coats streaked with tawny black that flickered like flames, with those short, curly heads that still seem those of wild bulls, those great fierce eyes, those sudden movements, and that edgy, jerky way of working that seems to resent the yoke and the goad and will obey any newly imposed domination only with a quiver of anger. These are what are called *freshly bound* oxen. The man in charge of them had to clear a corner of the field that had previously been abandoned as pasturage and filled with age-old tree stumps – a real athlete's task and one which his energy, his youth and his eight almost untamed animals between them were scarcely enough to accomplish.

A boy of between six and seven years of age, as pretty as an angel, wearing on his shoulders a lambskin that made him resemble the little John the Baptist depicted by Renaissance painters, was walking along the furrow parallel to the plough, and he was prodding the sides of the oxen with a long, light switch, armed with a not-too-sharp goad. The proud animals were quivering under the boy's light prods, and making the yokes and the straps attached to their brows creak, as they shook the shaft with their violent movements. Whenever a root got in the way of the ploughshare, the ploughman would cry out with a powerful voice, calling each animal by its name, but more to calm them down than to rouse them on; the oxen, irritated by this unexpected resistance, gave a start, dug up the earth with their broad cloven feet, and would have plunged off sideways, dragging the plough across the fields if the young man had not used his voice and his goad to keep the first four in place, while the boy managed the other four. He would cry out too, poor little chap, in a voice that he tried to make sound really threatening but that remained as gentle as his angelic face. The whole sight was beautiful in its strength or grace – the landscape, the man, the boy, the oxen under the yoke – and, in spite of this mighty struggle, in which the earth was vanquished, there was a feeling of mildness and deep calm hovering over all things. Once the obstacle had been surmounted and the team could resume its even and solemn march, the ploughman, whose feigned violence was merely a way of letting off steam and expending energy, would all at once resume the serenity of simple souls and glance across with paternal contentment at his boy, who turned round to smile at him. Then the masculine voice of that young paterfamilias would strike up the solemn and melancholy song that the ancient tradition of that region transmits, not to every ploughman without distinction, but to the ones who can most consummately spur on and sustain the ardour of the labouring oxen. This song, whose origin was perhaps considered sacred, and to which mysterious influences must once have been attributed, is even today still reputed to possess the virtue of ensuring these animals are always eager to work, of appeasing their discontent and filling with charm the tedium of their long chore. It is not enough to be able to guide them properly by tracing a perfectly straight furrow, to lighten their task by lifting the ploughshare or lowering it into the earth at just the right moment: you are not a perfect ploughman unless you can sing to the oxen, and this is a special art which requires a particular taste and skill.

This song is, in actual fact, merely a sort of recitative, interrupted and resumed at whim. Its irregular form and its intonations, false by the tenets of the art of music, make it untranslatable. But for all that, it remains a fine song, and it is so appropriate to the nature of the work that it accompanies, to the gait of the oxen, the calm of the rustic scene, and the simplicity of the men who intone it, that no genius foreign to the work of the fields could have invented it, and no singer other than a *skilful ploughman* of this region would be able to repeat it. At the times of the year when there is no other work and no other movement in the country than that of ploughing, this song, so gentle and so powerful, rises up like the voice of the breeze, to which its particular tonality gives it a certain resemblance. The final note of each phrase, held in a prolonged tremolo demanding incredible breath control, rises a quarter of a tone, systematically distorting the melody. It sounds wild, but its charm is inexpressible, and when you are used to hearing it, you cannot imagine another song being raised at these times and in these places, without disturbing their harmony.

So it was that I had before my eyes a picture that contrasted with Holbein's, though it was a similar scene. Instead of a sad old man, a young man, bright-eyed and bushy-tailed; instead of a team of emaciated and harassed horses, a double quadriga of robust and eager oxen; instead of Death, a charming boy; instead of an image of despair and an idea of destruction, a spectacle of energy and an idea of happiness.

It was then that the quatrain in French – *In the sweat of your brow, etc.,* – and the *'O fortunatos… agricolas'* of Virgil came back to my mind at the same time; and then – at the sight of this handsome couple, the man and the boy, carrying out in such poetic conditions, and with so much grace combined with so much vigour, a labour imbued with grandeur and solemnity – I felt a profound pity mingled with an unforced respect. Happy the ploughman! – Yes, doubtless, I would be happy in his place, if my arm, filled all of sudden with strength, and my lungs, filled with power, could in this way sing of nature and make it fecund, without my eyes ceasing to see or my brain to grasp the harmony of colours and sounds, the subtlety of tones and the graceful outlines of things – in a word, their mysterious beauty! And without, above all, my heart ceasing to be related to the divine feelings that presided over the whole immortal and sublime creation.

But alas! That man has never grasped the mystery of beauty, and that boy will never grasp it either!… God preserve me from thinking that they are no superior to the animals over which they have dominion, and that they do not have, for brief moments, a sort of ecstatic revelation that charms their fatigue and soothes their anxieties to sleep! I can see, set on their noble brows, the Lord's seal, for they are born kings of the earth, much more than are those who possess it because they have paid for it. And the proof that they can feel this is that they would resist any attempt to make them leave this land: they love this soil watered with their sweat, and the real peasant dies of homesickness when forced to wear a soldier's harness far from the field that saw his birth. But this man lacks a portion of the intense pleasures that I possess – immaterial pleasures that are really his due, as he is a worker in the vast temple that the sky is vast enough to enfold. What he lacks is an awareness of his feelings. Those who have condemned him to servitude from his mother's womb, unable to deprive him of his daydreams, have deprived him of self-conscious thought.

Well, just as he is, incomplete and condemned to an eternal childhood, he is yet a finer figure of a man than the one in whom knowledge has stifled all feeling. Do not raise yourselves above him, you who believe yourselves to be invested with the legitimate and inalienable right of telling him what to do, for that dreadful error into which you have fallen proves quite well enough that your minds have killed your hearts, and that you are the most incomplete and blindest of men!… I even prefer the simplicity of his soul to the fake enlightenment of yours, and if I had to tell his life story, I would enjoy bringing out the tender and touching aspects of it – enjoy it more than you gain any merit by depicting the abjection into which the rigours and disdain shown by your social precepts can plunge him.

I was acquainted with this young man and that handsome lad; I knew their story, since they had a story – everyone has a story (and everyone would be able to rouse interest in the novel of their own life, if they had really understood it…). Although he was a peasant and a simple ploughman, Germain had realised where his duties and his affections lay. He had narrated them to me, naively and clearly, and I had listened to him with interest. When I had watched him ploughing for quite some time, I asked myself why his story shouldn't get written down, even though it was quite a simple story, as straight and unadorned as the furrow that he traced out with his plough.

Next year, this furrow will be filled in and covered over by a new furrow. In the same way, the trace of most men in the field of humanity is marked out only to disappear. A clump of earth erases it, and the furrows that we have dug succeed one another like tombs in the cemetery. Isn't the ploughman's furrow of more value than that of the idler, even if the latter has made a name for himself – a name that will remain if, through some singularity or absurdity, he makes something of a noise in the world?…

Well, let us draw out of oblivion, if possible, the furrow made by Germain, the *skilful ploughman*. He won't know a thing about it and will barely worry his head over it, but the attempt will have given me a certain pleasure.

3

Père Maurice

'Germain,' his father-in-law said to him one day, 'you really must make up your mind about finding a new wife. You've been a widower for two years since you lost my daughter, and your older son is seven. You're coming up to thirty, my lad, and you know that once you've passed that age, round these parts, a man is considered too old to start a new household. You have three lovely children, and up until now they've been no bother to us. My wife and my daughter-in-law have looked after them as best they could, and loved them the way they should. Now Petit-Pierre's almost grown up; he can already prod the oxen along quite nicely; he's sensible enough to look after the animals in the meadow, and strong enough to lead the horses to water. So he's no bother, but the other two, though we love them well enough, God knows – well, those poor innocents are giving us a lot of worries this year. My daughter-in-law is ready to have her baby, and she's still got her arms full with the other little one. When the one we're expecting comes along, she won't be able to look after your little Solange and especially not your Sylvain – he's not four yet and he's into everything, night and day. He's a fidgety Philip like you; he'll make a good worker, but he's a real handful of a child, and my old woman can't run fast enough to catch up with him when he runs off out to the pond, or throws himself under the animals' hooves. And then, with the new one my daughter-in-law is bringing into the world, my wife's going to be lumbered with her last-but-one for a good year at least. So your children are a worry and a burden to us. We don't like to see children not being looked after properly; and when you think of all the accidents that can happen to them if you don't keep an eye on them, you can't have any peace of mind. So you need another wife and I need another daughter-in-law. Think about it, my lad. I've already warned you several times, the years won't wait for you. You owe it to yourself and to the rest of us – as we all want everything to go well at home – to get married as soon as you can.'

'Well, Father,' replied his son-in-law, 'if you absolutely insist, I'll have to do as you ask. But I don't want to conceal from you the fact that this will give me quite a headache, and as for wanting it, I'd almost as much drown myself. A man knows who he's lost and doesn't know who he's going to find. I had a fine wife, a lovely wife, sweet-tempered, hard-working, good to her father and mother, good to her husband, good to her children, good at work, both in the fields and in the home, nimble-fingered, good at everything, in short; and when you gave her to me, when I took her, we hadn't made it any part of our conditions that I'd ever forget her if I had the misfortune to lose her.'

'What you're saying comes from a kindly heart, Germain,' replied Père Maurice; 'I know that you loved my daughter, that you made her happy, and that if you could have satisfied Death by going in place of her, Catherine would be alive this very minute, and you'd be in the cemetery. She thoroughly deserved to be loved by you to that degree, and if you can't get over her loss, well, neither can we. But I don't mean to suggest you should forget her. The good Lord wanted her to leave us, and not a day goes by without our letting her know, through our prayers, our thoughts, our words and our actions, that we respect her memory and are sad she's gone. But if she could speak to you from the other world and tell you her wishes, she'd order you to look out for a mother for her little orphans. So you need to find a woman who's worthy to replace her. It's not going to be very easy, but it's not impossible, and when we've found one for you, you'll love her as much as you loved my daughter, since you're a decent chap, and you'll be grateful to her for doing us a favour and loving your children.'

'Very well, Father,' said Germain, 'I'll do your bidding as I always have done.'

'To do you justice, my son, you always have listened to the friendly and sensible reasons the head of the family has given you. So let's have a think together about the choice of your new wife. First, I don't think you should take any slip of a girl. That's not what you need. Girls are too flighty, and as it's quite a burden bringing up three children, especially when they come from a previous marriage, you would need a pretty kind-hearted and sensible soul, gentle, and very hard-working. If your wife isn't more or less the same age as you, she won't have much of a reason to take on a duty like that. She'll find you too old and your children too young. She'll moan, and your children will suffer.'

'That's just what's bothering me,' said Germain. 'What if the poor little dears were maltreated, hated, beaten?'

'God forbid!' replied the old man. 'But bad women are much rarer in our part of the world than good ones, and you'd need to be mad not to get your hands on the right one for you.'

'That's true, Father: there are some nice girls in our village. There's Louise, Sylvaine, Claudie, Marguerite… well, pretty much anyone you like.'

'Gently does it, my lad, all those girls are too young or too poor… or too pretty; after all, you need to think about that too, son. A pretty woman isn't always as well behaved as another.'

'You mean I should take an ugly one?' said Germain, sounding a bit worried.

'No, not ugly – this woman is going to give you some more children, and there's nothing so sad as having ugly children, ones that are weak and sickly. But a woman who's still fresh, in good health and neither beautiful nor ugly – she'd be just the thing for you.'

'I can see,' said Germain, smiling somewhat sadly, 'that if we're going to get the kind of woman you're after, we'll have to put her together ourselves – especially as you don't want her to be poor, and rich women aren't so easy to obtain, especially for a widower.'

'And what if she were a widow herself, Germain? What about it – a widow without any children but with a bit of property?'

'I can't think of any in our parish right now.'

'Me neither, but there are some in other places.'

'You've got someone in mind, Father, so tell me straight away.'

'Yes, I do have someone in mind,' replied Père Maurice. 'A certain Madame Léonard, Guérin's widow, living in Fourche.'

'I don't know the woman or the place,' replied Germain, in resigned but increasingly melancholy tones.

'Her name is Catherine, like your late lamented.'

'Catherine? Yes, it will be a pleasure for me to have that name to say: Catherine! And yet, if I can't love her as much as I did the other, it will be even more painful for me, it will remind me of her more often.'

'I can tell you that you *will* love her: she's a really nice person, a big-hearted woman; I haven't seen her for quite a while, she wasn't a plain Jane back then, but she's not so young now, she's thirty-two. She comes from a good family, they're all very decent folk, and she must have a good eight to ten thousand francs'-worth of land that she'd be happy to sell so as to buy new land wherever she settled down. She's thinking of getting married again too, you see, and I know that if your personality suited her, she wouldn't think your situation exactly unenviable.'

'So you've fixed it all up already?'

'Yes, apart from asking your and her opinions, and that's what you'd both need to ask one another, when you get acquainted. The woman's father is a distant relative of mine, and he's been a good friend to me. Old Père Léonard, I mean – do you know him well?'

'Yes, I've seen him talking to you at fairs, and at the last one you had lunch together; so that's what he was talking to you at such length about?'

'I guess so; he was watching you selling off your livestock and thought you gave a good account of yourself – he said you looked a sturdy lad, full of beans, with your head screwed on the right way; and when I'd told him all about you, and how nicely you've treated us in the eight years we've been living and working together, without a grumble or a cross word between us, he got it into his head to marry you off to his daughter; and that suits me too, I have to confess, given the fine reputation she has, her good, honest family, and the healthy business they're doing these days.'

'I can see, Father, that you take quite an interest in healthy business.'

'I suppose I do, yes. Don't you?'

'I can do if you want me to, if it gives you pleasure, but you know, as far as I'm concerned, I'm never all that fussed about what's mine and what isn't mine out of our profits. I'm not good at splitting it all up – I just can't get my head round that sort of thing. I know about land, oxen, horses, ploughing teams, seeding, threshing and forage. As for the sheep, the vines, the gardening, the minor profits and the quality farming, as you know, that's your son's affair, and I don't have that much to do with it. As for money, I don't have a long memory, and I'd rather hand it all over than have to quarrel over what's yours and what's mine. I'd be frightened of making a mistake and demanding what isn't my due, and if business wasn't plain and clear, I'd never get it sorted out.'

'That's too bad, son, and that's why I'd like you to have a wife with brains to replace me when I'm not here any more. You could never be bothered to look through our accounts properly, and that might cause a bit of inconvenience with my son, when the two of you don't have me around any more to smooth out any differences and tell you what belongs to each of you.'

'I hope you live a good long while yet, Father! But don't worry about what happens after you're gone; I'll never quarrel with your son. I trust Jacques just as I trust you, and since I don't have any property of my own, and everything that may fall to me comes from your daughter and belongs to our children, I can rest easy and so can you; Jacques wouldn't want to rob his sister's children for his own, since he loves them almost as much.'

'You're right as far as that goes, Germain. Jacques is a good son, a good brother and a man who loves the truth. But Jacques might die before you do, before your children have been reared, and you always need to remember, in a family, not to leave the minors without a head who can give them advice and settle their differences. Otherwise the lawyers stick their noses in, make them quarrel with one another and force them to squander all their money on lawsuits. And so we shouldn't think of bringing into our home an extra person, whether a man or a woman, without bearing in mind that one day that person will perhaps have to direct the conduct and the business of some thirty-odd children, grandchildren, sons-in-law and daughters-in-law… You never know how much a family is going to grow, and when the hive is too full and it's time to swarm, everyone thinks about making off with his own honey. When I took you as a son-in-law, although my daughter was rich and you were poor, I didn't criticise her in the slightest for having chosen you. I could see you were hard-working, and I was well aware that the richest possessions for country folk like us are a strong pair of arms and a heart like yours. When a man brings that into a family, he brings quite enough. But a woman's a different matter: her work in the home is good for maintaining things, not for acquiring them. In any case, now you're a father and looking for a wife, you need to remember that your new children, with nothing to lay claim to from the inheritance of the children from your first marriage, would find themselves in hardship if you happened to die, unless your wife had something put away on her own account. And then, the children you're going to provide for our colony will cost something to feed. If the responsibility fell on us alone, we'd feed them, that goes without saying, and without a single complaint, but the well-being of everybody would be lessened, and the first children would share in the deprivation. When families grow to an excessive size without their property growing in proportion, along comes hardship, however hard you work. Those are my observations, Germain: weigh them up, and see if you can't get widow Guérin to agree to you; after all, her good behaviour and her gold crowns will be helpful here in the present, and provide peace of mind for the future.'

'I hear you, Father. I'll try to get her to like me, and to like her myself.'

'For that you need to see her – to go and find her.'

'At her place? Fourche? It's quite a way from here, isn't it? And we hardly have time to go gadding about at this time of the year.'

'When it's a matter of a love marriage, you have to expect you'll waste time, but when it's a matter of a marriage of convenience between two people who are not inclined to whimsy and know what they want, it's soon decided. Tomorrow's Saturday; you can knock off early from the ploughing and leave about two o'clock after lunch; you'll be in Fourche by nightfall; it's a full moon right now, the roads are good, and it's no

21

more than three leagues away. It's near Magnier. Anyway, you can take the mare.'

'I'd just as soon go on foot, as it's a bit nippy.'

'Yes, but she's a fine mare, and a suitor who turns up on a fine mount makes a better impression. You can put your new suit on, and take a nice present of game for Père Léonard. You can say I sent you, and have a chat with him, you can spend all day Sunday with his daughter, and you'll be back with a yes or a no on Monday morning.'

'Fine,' Germain calmly replied.

And yet he wasn't altogether easy in his mind.

Germain had always led a sensible kind of life, like other hard-working peasants. Married at twenty, he had only ever loved one woman in his life, and since becoming a widower, although he was impetuous and jovial by nature, he had laughed and frolicked with no other. In his heart he really and truly missed her, and it was not without some fear and sadness that he was yielding to his father-in-law, but his father-in-law had always governed his family prudently, and Germain – who had dedicated himself to the common tasks, and consequently to the man who personified them, the father of the family – did not see how he could have demurred at such good reasons, against the interests of all.

Still, he was sad. Few days went by without him secretly weeping for his wife, and although solitude was starting to weigh on him, he was more scared at the idea of forming a new union than desirous of moving on from his sorrow. He kept telling himself, vaguely, that love might have been able to console him, if it had taken him unawares – for that is the only way that love *can* console. You don't find it if you start looking for it; it comes to us when we are least expecting it. This cold-blooded marriage plan that Père Maurice had set out before him, this unknown fiancée, and perhaps all the nice things said about her good sense and virtue were making him thoughtful. And off he went, mulling it over, as do men who do not have enough ideas for those ideas to compete with one another – in other words, unable to formulate for himself any good reasons for resistance and egotism, but suffering from a muffled sense of pain, while not struggling against the inevitable.

Meanwhile, Père Maurice had returned to the farm, while Germain, between sunset and nightfall, was busying the last hour of daylight repairing the breaches that the sheep had made in the hedge round a pen next to the farm buildings. He raised the stems of the thorns and propped them up with clods of earth, while the thrushes were twittering in the nearby bush and seemed to be urging him shrilly to hurry up, curious as they were to come and examine his work the minute he had left.

5

La Guillette

Père Maurice found at home an old neighbour woman who had come to have a chat with his wife while she fetched some embers to light her own fire. Mère Guillette lived in a very poor cottage two rifle-shots away from the farm. But she was a woman of order and strong will. Her poor house was clean and well maintained, and her clothes, carefully pieced together, expressed self-respect in the midst of her penury.

'So you've come for the evening fire, Mère Guillette,' the old man said to her. 'Anything else you want?'

'No, Père Maurice,' she replied; 'nothing at the minute. I'm not a scrounger, you know, and I don't over-rely on the kindness of my friends.'

'That's true; that way, your friends are always ready to do you a favour.'

'I was just having a chat with your wife, and I was asking her if Germain had finally made up his mind to get remarried.'

'You're not a chatterbox,' replied Père Maurice; 'we can tell you things without worrying about you spreading them: so I'll tell my wife and you that Germain's mind is well and truly made up, he's leaving tomorrow for the estate at Fourche.'

'Good for him!' exclaimed Mère Maurice; 'the poor lad! I hope to God he finds a wife as good and kind as he is!'

'Oh, so he's going to Fourche?' observed La Guillette. 'Now isn't that a coincidence! That really helps me out, and since you were asking me just now if there was anything I wanted, well, Père Maurice, I can tell you how you *can* help me, now you mention it.'

'Fire away – we're very happy to do you a favour.'

'If it's not too much trouble, I'd like Germain to take my daughter with him.'

'Where? To Fourche?'

'Not to Fourche, no; but to Les Ormeaux[6], where she'll be staying for the rest of the year.'

'What's this?' said Mère Maurice. 'Your daughter and you are going to live apart?'

'It's time for her to get a job and start earning. I'm not very happy about it and neither is she, poor soul! We couldn't take the step of separating at midsummer; now it's already autumn, and time for her to find a good position as a shepherdess in the farm at Les Ormeaux.[7] The farmer was passing by this way, only the other day, coming back from the fair. He saw my little Marie who was looking after her three sheep on the common.

' "You don't have a lot to do, little Miss," he said to her; "and three sheep, that's not much for a *shepherdlass*[8]. Would you like to look after a hundred? Come with me. Our shepherdess back home has fallen ill; she's heading back to her parents', and if you can be at ours before the week's out, you can have fifty francs for the rest of the year until midsummer."

'The girl turned his offer down, but she couldn't stop herself thinking about it and telling me all about it when she came home in the evening and saw me looking gloomy and worried about how to get through the winter; it's going to be a long, hard one – you can tell as, this year, we've seen the cranes and wild geese flying across the sky a good month earlier than usual. We both had a cry, but after a bit, we plucked up our courage. We told ourselves that we couldn't stay together, since there's hardly enough to keep a single person going on our little scrap of land, and now that Marie's grown up (she's turned sixteen), she really should do the same as the others, earn her crust and help her poor mother.'

'Mère Guillette,' the old ploughman said, 'if all it needed to console you for your sorrows and stop you having to send your daughter away was fifty francs, I promise I'd find it for you, even though fifty francs for folk like us is a pretty hefty sum. But in every situation we need to think about being sensible as well as friendly. It may protect you from the rigours of this winter, but not from the rigours that'll come after that, and the longer your daughter hesitates to make up her mind about a husband, the more both she and you will find it difficult to leave each other. Little Marie is getting to be big and strong, and there isn't enough to keep her busy at your place. She might start getting into lazy ways…'

'Oh, I'm not worried she'll do that,' said La Guillette. 'Marie's as hard-working as any rich girl in charge of a big job can be. She doesn't sit still with her arms folded for a single minute, and when we don't have any work on, she cleans and polishes our poor old furniture – you can see your own reflection in it. She's worth her weight in gold, is that child, and I'd much rather she'd gone to yours as a shepherdess rather than going all that way to people I don't know. You could have taken her on at midsummer, if we'd been able to make our minds up, but you've already hired everyone you need, and we won't be able to think about that possibility until midsummer next year.'

'Oh, I'll agree to that with all my heart, Guillette! It'll be a pleasure for me. But meanwhile, it'll be a good idea for her to learn a job and get used to working for other people.'

'Yes, I suppose so; anyway, it's all decided. The farmer from Les Ormeaux asked for her this morning; we said yes, and she's got to go. But the poor lass doesn't know the way, and I wouldn't like to send her that far all by herself. Since your son-in-law is going to Fourche tomorrow, he can take her with him. I gather it's right next to the estate where she's heading, or so I've been told; I've never actually been that way myself.'

'It's right next door, and my son-in-law will take her. It's the best solution; he'll even be able to take her behind the saddle on the mare, which will keep her shoes clean. Look, he's just coming in for supper. Listen, Germain, Mère Guillette's little Marie is off to be a shepherdess at Les Ormeaux. You can take her on your horse, can't you?'

'Of course,' said Germain, slightly anxious but always ready to help out his neighbour.

In our world, such a thing would never enter a mother's head – entrusting a sixteen-year-old girl to a twenty-eight-year-old man; for Germain was in fact only twenty-eight, and although, by the standards of his region, he was considered an old man from the marriage point of view, he was still the handsomest man in the locality. Work had not made him gaunt and withered as it had the majority of peasants with ten years' ploughing on their backs. He was strong enough to carry on at the plough for another ten years without seeming old, and a prejudice against his greater age would have had to be strong indeed in the mind of a young girl if it had prevented her from seeing that Germain was fresh-complexioned, with eyes as sparkling and blue as a sky in May, pink lips, superb teeth and a body as elegant and supple as that of a young horse which has yet to leave the meadow.

But a chaste lifestyle is a sacred tradition in certain country regions, far away as they are from the corrupt bustle of the big cities, and, among all the families of Belair, Maurice's family had the reputation of being decent and truthful. Germain was heading off to seek a wife; Marie was a girl, too young and too poor for him to think about her in that way, and unless he'd been a *heartless man*, a *bad man*, it was impossible for him to have entertained a single guilty thought about her. So Père Maurice was not in the least worried to see him with that pretty girl riding behind him in the saddle; La Guillette would have been considered to be insulting him if she had asked him to respect Marie like a sister; Marie mounted the mare weeping, after hugging her mother and her girlfriends twenty times over. Germain, who had his own reasons for being sad, felt all the more sympathy for her sorrow, and set off with a serious expression on his face, while the folk from the neighbourhood waved poor Marie goodbye without imagining anything untoward might happen.

6

Petit-Pierre

Grey was a young, beautiful and sturdy beast. She bore her double burden effortlessly, flattening her ears and champing at the bit, like the proud and ardent mare she was. As she passed by the long meadow, she spotted her mother, whose name was Old Grey just as hers was Young Grey, and she whinnied a farewell. Old Grey trotted up to the hedge, her hobbles rattling, and tried to gallop along the edge of the meadow to follow her daughter, but, seeing her starting to canter, she whinnied in turn, and stayed pensive, anxious, sniffing the wind, her mouth filled with the grass that she had stopped chewing.

'The poor beast still recognises her offspring,' said Germain to take Marie's mind off her sorrows. 'That reminds me: I didn't give my Petit-Pierre a hug before leaving. The wretched child wasn't there! Yesterday evening, he wanted me to promise I'd take him, and he cried for a whole hour in his bed. Then again this morning, he tried everything to persuade me. Oh, he's a sly one, a little wheedler! But when he saw it was out of the question, the young sir got cross; he went out into the fields, and I didn't see him all day.'

'But *I* saw him,' said little Marie, trying to hold back her tears. 'He was running with the Soulas children out towards the coppice, and I suspected he'd been out of the house for quite some time, since he was hungry and was eating sloes and blackberries off the bushes. I gave him the bit of bread I had for my snack, and he said, "Thanks, my darling little Marie; when you come to ours, I'll give you some *galette*⁹". He's just such a sweetie, that lad of yours, Germain!'

'Yes, he's a sweetie,' replied the ploughman, 'and I don't think there's anything I wouldn't do for him! If his grandmother hadn't been more sensible than me, I wouldn't have been able to leave him behind, when I saw him crying so much his poor little heart was all swollen.'

'Well, why shouldn't you have brought him along, Germain? He wouldn't have been much trouble to you; he's so sensible when people do as he wants them to!'

'Seems he'd have been in the way where I'm going. Least, that was Père Maurice's view… In *my* opinion, I'd have imagined it would be a good idea to see what kind of a welcome they gave him, and I'm sure such a nice lad could only have been treated in the most friendly way… But they say at home that we shouldn't start off by showing them what a big responsibility the household will be… I don't know why I'm telling you all this, young Marie; you don't understand.'

'Oh yes I do, Germain; I know you're going there to get married again; my mother told me, and went on about how I shouldn't mention it to anyone, neither at yours, nor at the place I'm going to, and you can rest assured, I won't breathe a word.'

'You'd better not, since it's not settled; maybe I won't be right for the woman in question.'

'Let's hope you will, Germain. Why wouldn't you be right for her?'

'Who knows? I've got three children, and it's a heavy burden for a woman who isn't their mother!'

'That's true, but your children aren't like other children.'

'Do you think so?'

'They're as lovely as little angels, and so well brought up that everyone says you couldn't wish to see any nicer children.'

'There's Sylvain, he can be a bit of a handful.'

'He's only little! Of course he's going to be a little terror, but he's so clever!'

'It's true he's clever – and brave with it! He's not afraid of cows, or bulls, and if he was left to his own devices, he'd already be climbing onto horses with his older brother.'

'If I were you, I'd have brought the older one along. You can be sure she'd have loved you straight away for having such a fine boy!'

'Yes, if the woman likes children, but what if she doesn't?'

'Are there *any* women who don't like children?'

'Not many, I don't think, but anyway, there are a few, and that's what's bothering me.'

'So you don't know this woman at all, then?'

'No more than you do, and I'm afraid I may not know her any better even when I've seen her. I'm not the suspicious type. When people say nice things to me, I believe them, but I've been on the point of regretting it more than once, since words aren't the same as deeds.'

'They say she's a really nice woman.'

'Who says that? Père Maurice?'

'Yes, your father-in-law.'

'That's all very well, but he doesn't know her either.'

'Well, you'll be seeing her soon, you can have a good look from up close, and let's hope you don't get it wrong, Germain.'

'Listen, young Marie, I'd be really grateful if you'd come into the house with me, rather than head straight off to Les Ormeaux: you're smart, you've always shown how bright you are, and you pick up on everything. If you see something that makes you have second thoughts, you can have a quiet word with me.'

'Oh no, Germain, I won't do that! I'd be too afraid of getting it wrong, and anyway, if a hasty word was to put you off this marriage, your parents would be cross with me, and I've already got quite enough problems as it is, without causing any more for my poor old mother, the dear woman.'

As they were talking, Grey shied, and pricked up her ears, then came back on her tracks and went over to the bush, where something that she was now starting to recognise had at first frightened her. Germain glanced over to the bush, and saw in the ditch, under the thick, still-fresh foliage of the main branch of a thinned-out oak tree, something that he took for a lamb.

'It's an animal that's got lost,' he said, 'or maybe it's dead, since it's not moving. Perhaps someone's searching for it; we'd better take a look!'

'It's not an animal!' exclaimed little Marie; 'it's a child asleep; it's your little Petit-Pierre.'

'Well, what the…!' said Germain, jumping off his horse; 'just look at the little rascal asleep there, so far away from home, in a ditch where a snake might easily find him!'

He took the child up in his arms. The boy smiled at him as he opened his eyes and threw his arms round his neck, saying to him:

'Oh Daddy, you're going to take me with you!'

'Oh yes, always the same old song! What were you doing there, you naughty little Pierre?'

'I was waiting for my daddy to come by,' said the child. 'I was keeping an eye on the path, and after watching for a while I fell asleep.'

'And what if I'd gone by without seeing you? You'd have spent the whole night out of doors, and the wolf would have gobbled you up!'

'Oh, I just knew you'd see me!' replied Petit-Pierre confidently.

'Well, right now, young Pierre, give me a hug, say goodbye, and hurry along home if you don't want them to have supper without you.'

'So aren't you going to take me along with you?' exclaimed the boy, starting to rub his eyes to show that he was deliberately going to start crying.

'You know perfectly well that Grandfather and Grandmother don't want you to,' said Germain, sheltering behind the authority of the grandparents, like a man who can hardly depend on his own.

But the child refused to listen. He started to cry for real, saying that since his father was taking little Marie along, he could just as well take *him*. He was told by way of objection that they'd have to go through the big woods, where there'd be lots of wicked beasts who ate up little children; Grey wouldn't want to carry three people, she'd said as much when they set off, and in the part of the world where they were going to, there was neither a bed nor any supper for kids. All these excellent reasons failed to persuade Petit-Pierre; he threw himself on the grass, and rolled around on it, crying that his daddy didn't love him any more, and that unless he took him along with him, he wouldn't go back home, whether it was night or day.

Germain had a father's heart as tender and feeble as that of a woman. The death of his wife, the way he had been forced to look after his children all by himself, as well as the thought that those poor motherless children needed a lot of love, had all contributed to making him like that, and he was so torn apart inside – all the more since he blushed at his weakness and had to struggle to hide his unease from little Marie – that his forehead broke out into a sweat and his eyes grew red rimmed, being on the point of shedding tears too. Finally he tried to get angry; but, turning to little Marie, as if to demonstrate clearly his firmness of soul to her, he saw that the kindly girl's face was bathed in tears, and all his courage abandoned him; it was impossible for him to hold back his own tears, even though he continued to grumble and threaten.

'True, you're too hard-hearted,' little Marie finally said to him, 'and if you ask me, I'll never be able to resist a child who's so upset, the way that you do. Go on, Germain, just take him with you. Your mare is perfectly used to carrying two grown-ups and a child – after all, your brother-in-law and his wife, who's a lot heavier than me, go off to market with their boy on the back of this good beast. You can put him on the horse in front of you, and anyway, I'd rather go along on foot all by myself than upset the lad.'

'That's as maybe,' replied Germain, who was dying to give in. 'Grey is strong and could carry two more, if there was room on her back. But what are we going to do with the boy on the journey? He'll be cold, he'll be hungry… And who'll look after him this evening and tomorrow – who'll put him to bed, give him a wash and get him dressed? I don't dare give this job to a woman I don't know – one who'll probably think, I don't doubt, that I'm hardly getting off to a good start, treating her so casual-like.'

'Depending on whether she seems friendly or annoyed, you'll know straight away what kind of a person she is, Germain – believe you me. And anyway, if she turns your Pierre away, I can look after him. I'll go to hers to get him dressed and I'll take him out into the fields tomorrow. I'll keep him happy all day long and I'll make sure that he doesn't go short of anything.'

'And he'll be a real nuisance to you, poor lass! He'll be under your feet! A whole day, that's a long time!'

'No, not at all, I'll enjoy it; it'll be company for me, and it'll make my first day in a new part of the world less sad. I'll imagine that I'm still at yours.'

The boy, seeing that little Marie was taking his side, was clinging to her skirts and holding on so tight that they'd have had to hurt him to drag him away. When he realised his father was giving in, he took Marie's hand in his own two little hands, tanned brown in the sunshine, and kissed it, leaping with joy and pulling her over to the mare, with the impatient ardour that children show in their desires.

'Come now,' said the young girl, lifting him up in her arms, 'let's try to calm down this poor heart that's skipping like a little bird, and if you feel the cold when night falls, just you tell me, young Pierre; I'll keep you nice and snug in my cape. Give your daddy a kiss, and tell him you're sorry for being naughty. Say it won't happen again, never! Never – do you hear?'

'Yes, yes, but only so long as I always do what he wants me to, is that it?' said Germain, wiping the boy's eyes with his handkerchief. 'Ah, Marie! You're spoiling the young rascal… And you really are just too kind, young Marie. I don't know why you didn't come and work as a shepherdess for us last midsummer. You could have kept an eye on my children, and I'd have preferred to pay you a good wage for looking after them, rather than going off to look for a wife who maybe will think she's doing me a huge favour just by not hating them.'

'You mustn't look at things in the wrong light,' replied Marie, holding the horse's bridle while Germain placed his son on the front of the broad packsaddle covered with goatskin. 'If your wife doesn't like children, you can take me into your service next year, and, you can rest assured, I'll keep them so busy and cheerful that they won't notice a thing.'

7

In the Moors

'Hang on,' said Germain, when they had taken a few steps, 'what are they going to think back home when this little chap doesn't turn up? His grandparents are going to be worried and they'll start looking everywhere for him.'

'You can go and tell the road-mender working up there on the road that you're taking him with you, and ask him to go and tell your family.'

'That's true, Marie, you think of everything, you do; I'd quite forgotten that Jeannie would be round these parts.'

'Yes, and what's more, he lives right near the farm; he won't forget to carry out the errand.'

When they'd thought of this precaution, Germain set the mare trotting, and Petit-Pierre was so delighted that he did not at first realise that he hadn't had any dinner, but the horse's movement left him feeling hollow in the pit of his stomach, and after a league, he started to yawn, to turn pale and to confess that he was starving hungry.

'Now it's starting!' said Germain. 'I knew all along that we wouldn't get far without young sir starting to moan about being hungry or thirsty.'

'I'm thirsty as well!' said Petit-Pierre.

'All right, we'll go into the inn run by Mère Rebec in Corlay, the *Break of Day*! A nice name for an inn, but not much of a place to stay! Come on, Marie, you can drink a drop of wine too.'

'No, no, I don't need anything,' she said, 'I'll hold the mare while you go in with the lad.'

'But now I think about it, my dear, this morning you gave the bread from your snack to my Pierre, and you haven't had a bite to eat; you didn't want to have any dinner with us at home, you were too busy crying.'

'Oh, I wasn't hungry, I was too upset! And I swear to you that even now I really don't feel like having anything to eat.'

'You need to force yourself, my lass, otherwise you'll be ill. We still have quite a way to go, and we mustn't arrive there looking famished and as if we'd turned up to ask for bread even before saying hello.

Follow my example, even though I don't have much of an appetite; but I'll force myself to do it, since, after all, I didn't have any dinner either. I was watching you and your mother crying, and it made me feel all bothered inside. Come on, I'll tie Grey to the door; get down now, do as I tell you.'

All three of them went into Rebec's place, and in less than a quarter of an hour, the big lame woman managed to rustle up a decent-looking omelette, with some wholemeal bread and some local light red wine.

Peasants do not rush their food, and little Pierre had such a big appetite that a whole hour went by before Germain could think about resuming their journey. Little Marie had eaten to please him, at first; then, little by little, she had started to feel hungry; after all, at sixteen, you can't go without food for very long, and the air of the countryside has a powerful effect. The kindly words that Germain found to console her and make her buck up also did their bit; she made an effort to persuade herself that seven months would soon have gone by, and to think of how happy she would be at finding herself back in her own family and her own hamlet, since Père Maurice and Germain had come to an agreement and promised to take her on. But just as she was starting to cheer up and chat to little Pierre, Germain had the unfortunate idea of pointing out to her, through the tavern window, the fine view over the valley, that can be seen in its entirety from this height, in all its green and fertile loveliness. Marie looked, and asked if, from here, they could see the houses of Belair.

'I should think so,' said Germain, 'and the farm, and even your house. Look, that little grey dot, not far from Godard's big poplar – down a bit from the church steeple.'

'Oh! I can see it!' said the girl, and immediately started crying again.

'It was wrong of me to make you remember that,' said Germain. 'I'm doing some stupid things today! Come on, Marie, let's be off, my dear; the days are short, and in one hour, when the moon rises, it won't be so warm.'

They set off again, crossing the great *heathland*[10], and since, so as not to overtire the young girl and the little boy by trotting along too fast, Germain could hardly make Grey go all that quickly, the sun had set by the time they left the road and headed into the woods.

Germain knew the route as far as Magny, but he reflected that he could take a short cut if he avoided the Chanteloube path and went down along by Presles and La Sépulture, a route he was not in the habit of taking when he went to the fair. He got lost and wasted a bit more time before entering the wood, and then, without realising it, he did not enter it on the side he should have. As a result, he turned away from Fourche and came to a much higher spot on the Ardentes side.

What at first prevented him from finding his bearings was a mist that rose with the night, one of those autumn evening mists that the white gleam of the moonlight makes even more hazy and deceptive. The great puddles that dot the clearings gave off such thick vapours that, when Grey walked through these puddles, they realised she was doing so only because of the lapping of the water at her feet and the difficulty she had in extricating her hooves from the mud.

It was only when they had finally found a nice straight path and reached the end of it, and Germain could look round to see where they were, that he realised he was lost, for Père Maurice, when he had been explaining which way to go, had told him that as he came out of the woods he would have to make his way down quite a steep slope, cross a huge meadow and ford the river twice. He had even recommended that he take care on entering this river, since at the start of the season there had been heavy rainfall and the water level could be quite high. On seeing neither a downward slope, nor a meadow, nor a river, but the moor all smooth and white like an unbroken layer of snow, Germain halted, looked for a house, waited for someone to pass by, and found nothing that could give him any help. So he retraced his steps and entered the woods. But the mist grew even thicker, the moon was entirely hidden by the clouds, the paths were dreadfully rough and the potholes deep. Twice in succession, Grey almost stumbled and fell; heavily laden as she was, she was starting to lose heart, and while she still had enough discernment not to bump into the trees, she could not prevent the passengers on her back from having to cope with the big branches barring the way at head height – very dangerous they were. Germain lost his hat in one of these encounters and found it again only with the greatest difficulty. Petit-Pierre had gone off to sleep, and, letting himself flop forward like a sack, he curled up in a heap in his father's arms, so that Germain could neither keep the horse going nor guide it in the right direction.

'I think we're bewitched,' said Germain, coming to a halt. 'These woods aren't big enough to get lost in, unless you're drunk, and we've been going round in them for at least two hours without being able to get out. Grey has only one idea in her head: going back home. And she's the one who's leading me astray. If we *do* want to go back home, we need only to let her follow her nose. But when we're perhaps only a hop and a skip away from the place we're supposed to be sleeping in, we'd have to be mad to give up and start out on such a long road all over again. Still, I really don't know what to do any more. I can't see either sky or ground, and I'm afraid this boy might catch a fever if we stay out in this damn mist, or else he might get crushed by our weight if the horse happens to fall forwards.'

'There's no point in trying to press on,' said little Marie. 'Let's get down, Germain; give me the boy, I'll easily be able to carry him, and I'm better placed than you to stop the cape from falling open and leaving him unprotected. You can lead the mare by the bridle, and perhaps we'll have a clearer idea of where we are when we're closer to the ground.'

This did at least protect them from falling off the horse, but that was the only advantage, since the mist was creeping along and seemed to be sticking to the damp earth. It was difficult to walk, and they were soon so perplexed that they decided to halt when they finally came across a dry spot under some great oak trees. Little Marie was dripping with sweat, but she did not complain or worry about a thing. All her thoughts were for the child, and she sat down on the sand and laid him on her knees, while Germain explored the environs, after tying Grey's reins round a branch.

But Grey, who was getting very fed up with this whole trip, shook her haunches, pulled off the reins, broke the straps, and, rearing up high into the air a good half-dozen times by way of farewell, galloped off through the undergrowth, showing all too clearly that she did not need anyone else to show her the way home.

'Well!' said Germain, after chasing after her for a while in vain, 'here we are on foot, and even if we found the right path, it wouldn't be any use, since we'd need to cross the river on foot too; and seeing how all these routes are waterlogged, we can be sure that the meadow is submerged. We don't know the other paths through. So we'll just have to wait until this mist lifts; it can't last more than another hour or two. When we can see clearly, we'll look for a house, the first one we come to on the edge of the wood; but right now we can't get out of here; there's a pond or a little lake, goodness knows what ahead of us; and behind us, I wouldn't be able to say what there is either – I've completely lost track of which way we came.'

'Never mind, let's just be patient, Germain,' said little Marie. 'It's not so bad on this little rise. The rain can't get in through the leaves of these big oak trees, and we can light a fire – I can feel some old tree stumps that won't be too difficult to pull out and are dry enough to catch fire. You have a light, don't you, Germain? You were smoking your pipe just now.'

'I *did* have a light! My flint was on the packsaddle in my bag, with the game birds I was taking along for my future wife, but that cursed mare has run off with it all, even my coat – she's bound to ruin it, getting it torn on all the branches.'

'No, Germain, look: the old packsaddle, the coat, the bag, they're all there, on the ground at your feet. Grey broke the straps and threw it all down next to her when she ran off.'

'Good Lord, you're quite right!' said the ploughman; 'and if we can feel around and pick up a bit of dead wood, we'll be able to get ourselves dry and warm.'

'That's not very difficult,' said little Marie; 'there's dead wood crackling underfoot wherever we step; but just hand me over the packsaddle first.'

'What do you want to do with it?'

'Make a bed for the youngster – no, not like that, the other way round; he won't roll out of it that way, and it's still nice and warm from the beast's back. Wedge it in on each side, please, with the stones you can see just there!'

'I can't see them! You must have the eyes of a cat!'

'There we are! All done, Germain! Give me your coat, so I can wrap up his little feet, and my cape over his body. Look! Don't you think he's as nice and snug there as in his own bed! And feel how warm he is!'

'True! You're good at looking after children, Marie!'

'You don't need any magic tricks for that. Now get your flint out of your bag, and I'll go and sort out the wood.'

'This wood will never catch, it's too damp.'

'You make difficulties over everything, Germain! So don't you remember when you were a shepherd boy and you lit great fires in the fields, in the middle of the pouring rain?'

'Yes, it's a talent that you pick up when you're a child looking after the animals, but I was a cattle drover as soon as I could walk.'

'That's why you're stronger in the arm than clever with your hands. There: our fire's all ready, just see if it doesn't catch! Give me your flint and a handful of dry fern. That's the way! Now blow; you're not weak in the lungs?'

'Not as far as I know,' said Germain, blowing like a forge bellows.

After a moment, the flame shone, first shedding a red light, and finally rising in bluish spurts under the oaks' foliage, repelling the mist and gradually drying up the atmosphere for ten feet around.

'Now I'm going to sit next to the youngster to make sure no sparks fall on his body,' said the girl. 'You can add wood and keep the fire going, Germain! We won't be picking up a fever or a cold here, Germain, I can promise you.'

'My word, but you're a clever girl,' said Germain, 'and you can get a fire going like a real little night witch. I'm starting to buck up a bit, and I reckon I can face things better now. With my legs soaked up to my knees, and the idea of having to stay like that until daybreak, I was in a pretty bad mood just now.'

'And when people get into a bad mood, they can't think straight,' replied little Marie.

'And so *you* never get into a bad mood, I take it?'

'No, never! What good does it do?'

'Oh it doesn't do any good, I grant you, but it's difficult not to, when troubles come along! And yet, God knows, you've had a few troubles of your own, my poor lass – it hasn't always been easy for you!'

'True, we've had our share of suffering, my poor mother and me. We had our trials and tribulations, but we never lost heart.'

'I'd never lose heart either, not over anything,' said Germain, 'but poverty would get me down – I've never gone short. My wife had made me wealthy, and I still am; I always will be, as long as I work at the farm – for ever, I hope. But we all have our burdens to bear! I've suffered in other ways.'

'Yes, you lost your wife, and that's just so sad!'

'It is, isn't it?'

'Oh, I cried so much for her, you know, Germain! She was so nice and kind! Look, let's not talk about it any more; I'd start crying for her all over again – all my sad thoughts are coming back to me today.'

'It's true she loved you a lot, little Marie! She thought the world of you and your mother. Oh come on – are you crying? Look, lass, I don't want to start crying too…'

'But you *are* crying, Germain! You're crying too! Where's the shame in a man crying for his wife? Don't hold it back, go ahead! A burden shared is a burden halved!'

'You have a kindly heart, Marie, and it does me good to have a bit of a cry with you. But stretch your feet out to the fire; your skirt's all wet too, you poor thing! Look, I'll take over with the youngster, just you warm yourself up a bit.'

'I'm warm enough,' said Marie, 'and if you want to sit down, take a corner of the coat – I'm fine as it is.'

'As a matter of fact, it's not so bad being here,' said Germain, sitting right next to her. 'The one thing that's really niggling me is how hungry I am. It must be nine o'clock, and I found it so difficult struggling along those lousy paths that I feel quite giddy. Aren't you a bit hungry too, Marie?'

'Me? Not at all. I'm not in the habit of having four meals a day like you, and I've gone to bed without supper so many times that once more will hardly make much of a difference.'

'Ah, it's really convenient having a woman like you around; you don't cost much,' said Germain, with a smile.

'I'm not a woman,' said Marie, naively, not noticing the turn the ploughman's ideas had taken. 'Are you dreaming?'

'Yes, I think I am dreaming,' replied Germain; 'it's the hunger that's making my mind wander, perhaps!'

'What a greedy-guts you are!' she replied, brightening up in her turn. 'Well, if you can't live for five or six hours without eating, don't you have some game in that bag of yours, and a fire to cook it on?'

'Damn it, that's a good idea! But what about my future father-in-law's present?'

'You've got six partridges and a hare! I don't think you're going to need all that to fill you up?'

'But if I cook it here, without a skewer or any fire-dogs, it'll turn into charcoal!'

'No,' said little Marie; 'let me do it, I'll cook it under the ashes so it doesn't even taste of smoke. Haven't you ever caught skylarks out in the country, and cooked them up between a couple of stones? Oh, it's true – I'd forgotten you were never a shepherdlad! Anyway, pluck this partridge! Don't tear at it now, you'll pull all the skin off!'

'You might pluck the other one to give me an idea!'

'So you want to eat two, do you? What an ogre! Look, there they are, all plucked, now I can cook them.'

'You'd make a perfect canteen-keeper, young Marie; unfortunately you don't have a canteen, and I'll be reduced to drinking the water out of this pool.'

'You'd like some wine, wouldn't you? Perhaps you could really do with a coffee? You must think you're at the fair, relaxing under the leafy arbour! Call the tavern-keeper – some liqueur for the skilful ploughman of Belair!'

'Ah, you little scamp, are you making fun of me? Wouldn't *you* drink some wine if you had some, then?'

'Me? I drank some with you that evening at Mère Rebec's place, for the second time in my life; but if you're good, I'll give you a bottle that's almost full – good stuff, too!'

'How come, Marie? You really must be a witch!'

'Weren't you so extravagant as to ask Rebec for two bottles of wine? You drank one with your lad, and I hardly swallowed three drops of the one you'd placed in front of me. But you'd paid for both of them without thinking.'

'And so?'

'And so I put the one that hadn't been drunk into my basket, since I thought either you or your lad would get thirsty on the journey, and here it is.'

'You're the most sensible girl I've ever met. Just think – even though she was crying, poor lass, when she came out of the inn, even that didn't stop her thinking of others more than of herself. Poor Marie, the man who marries you will certainly be no fool.'

'I hope so – I wouldn't like a fool. Come on now, eat up your partridges, they're done to a turn; and as there's no bread, you can make do with chestnuts.'

'And where the devil did you get chestnuts from?'

'You'd never believe me! All along the way, I picked them off the branches as I went by, and filled my pockets with them.'

'And they're cooked too?'

'And what a numbskull I'd have been if I hadn't thought to put the chestnuts in the fire the minute it was lit! That's what we always do out in the fields.'

'Ah, little Marie! We're going to have supper together! I want to drink to your health and hope you get a fine husband… there, just the kind you'd wish for yourself. Tell me what kind you'd like!'

'I'd find that very difficult, Germain, seeing as I've never given it a thought.'

'What, not at all? Never?' said Germain, starting to eat with a ploughman's appetite, but cutting off the best bits to offer them to his companion, who obstinately refused them, and contented herself with a few chestnuts. 'So tell me, young Marie,' he resumed, seeing she was not answering him, 'haven't you had any thoughts about marriage yet? You're the right age, you know!'

'Perhaps,' she said; 'but I'm too poor. You need at least a hundred crowns to settle down with someone, and I need to work for five or six years to save that much.'

'Poor girl! I wish Père Maurice would give *me* a hundred crowns, then I could make you a present of them.'

'Thanks a lot, Germain. And whatever would people say of me?'

'What do you want them to say? Everyone knows I'm old and can't marry you. So nobody would get the idea that I… that you…'

'Just a minute, old ploughman! Your boy's just waking up,' said little Marie.

Petit-Pierre had lifted himself up and was looking around pensively.

'Oh, he *always* does that when he hears people eating, little scamp!' said Germain. 'The noise of a cannon couldn't wake him, but when anyone starts munching and crunching near him, he opens his eyes straight away.'

'You must have been like that at his age,' said little Marie, with a sly smile. 'Well now, young Pierre, are you looking for the tester over your bed? It's made of twigs and leaves this evening, my lad, but that hasn't stopped your father having his supper. Would you like to have supper with him? I haven't eaten your share; I knew very well that you'd be wanting it!'

'Marie, I insist you eat,' exclaimed the ploughman, 'I won't have any more. I'm a rude, greedy fellow; you're going without your share for us, and that's not fair – I'm ashamed. Look, that's taken the edge off my appetite; I don't want my son to have supper unless you do too.'

'Leave us alone,' replied little Marie, '*you* don't hold the key to our appetites. Mine is closed today, but your Pierre's is open like a little wolf's. Just look at him tuck in! Oh, he's going to be a sturdy ploughman too!'

And Petit-Pierre was indeed showing he was his father's son, and despite being barely awake, not understanding where he was, nor how he had got there, he started to gobble down the food. Then, when his appetite was satisfied, he found he was as excited as all children whose habits have been disturbed; he showed more intelligence, more curiosity and more good sense than usual. He had them explain where he was, and when he realised it was in the middle of a wood, he felt rather afraid.

'Are there fierce animals in this wood?' he asked his father.

'No,' said his father, 'there aren't any. There's nothing to be afraid of.'

'So you were lying to me when you told me that if I went with you into the big woods the wolves would carry me off?'

'He's a logical chap, isn't he?' said Germain, embarrassed.

'He's right,' replied little Marie, 'you did say that to him – he's got a good memory, he hasn't forgotten. But you ought to learn, young Pierre, that your father never tells a lie. We came through the big woods while you were asleep, and now we're in the little woods, where there aren't any fierce animals.'

'Are the little woods very far away from the big ones?'

'Quite far; but anyway, the wolves don't come out of the big woods. And then, if any of them did come here, your father would kill them.'

'And you would too, little Marie?'

'And we would too – you'd help us of course, my little Pierre? You're not scared, are you? You'd give them a great thwack!'

'Yes, yes!' said the emboldened child, striking a heroic pose, 'we'd kill them!'

'There's no one as good as you at talking to children,' Germain told little Marie, 'and getting them to be sensible. Admittedly, you were a small child yourself not all that long ago, and you can remember what your mother used to say to you. I really think that the younger anyone is, the better they can get on with other young people. I'm really afraid a thirty-year-old woman who doesn't yet know what it means to be a mother will find it difficult to chat to kids and get them to be sensible.'

'Why ever not, Germain? I don't know why you're thinking bad things about that woman. You'll come round to her!'

'Devil take the woman!' said Germain. 'I wish I *had* come round and never needed to go back to her. What need do I have of a woman I don't even know?'

'But Daddy,' said the boy, 'why are you still talking about your wife today, since she's dead?…'

'Oh dear – so haven't you forgotten her then, your poor dear mother?'

'No, since I saw them put her in a lovely white wooden box, and my grandmother took me up to kiss her and say goodbye to her!… She was all white and cold, and every evening my aunt makes me say my prayers to the Lord so that she can go and get nice and warm with Him in heaven. Do you think she's there now?'

'I hope so, son, but you need to carry on praying; it'll show your mother that you love her.'

'I *will* say my prayers,' said the boy. 'I forgot to say them this evening.

45

But I can't say them all by myself; I always forget some of the words. Little Marie will have to help me.'

'Yes, Pierre, I'll help you,' the young girl said. 'Come over here, kneel down on me.'

The boy knelt down on the young girl's skirt, put his little hands together, and started to recite his prayers, at first attentively and fervently, since he knew the beginning very well, then more slowly and hesitantly, and finally repeating verbatim the words that little Marie dictated to him when he reached that part of his prayer where, as he was overcome by sleep at just that point every evening, he had never been able to learn it right to the end. Again, this time, the effort of attention and the monotony of his own accent produced their habitual effect, and it was only with difficulty that he could pronounce the final syllables, and even then he had to have them repeated three times over to him; his head grew heavy and leaned on Marie's chest; his hands relaxed, separated and fell wide open onto his knees. By the light of the fire of the bivouac, Germain gazed at his little angel dozing on the young girl's heart; she, holding him in her arms and warming his blond hair with her pure breath, had also drifted off into a pious reverie, and was silently praying for Catherine's soul.

Germain was touched, and tried to think what he could tell young Marie that would express the esteem and gratitude she inspired within him, but he could find nothing that would translate his thoughts. He came over to her to kiss his son whom she was still holding pressed against her breast, and he had to force himself to pull his lips away from little Pierre's forehead.

'You're kissing him too hard,' said Marie to him, gently pushing the ploughman's head away, 'you'll wake him up. Let me lay him down again, since he's set off again for his dreams of paradise.'

The boy allowed himself to be laid down, but as he stretched out on the goatskin of the packsaddle, he asked if he was on Grey. Then, opening his big blue eyes, and staring fixedly at the branches for a minute, he seemed to be dreaming while still wide awake, or to have been struck by an idea that had slipped into his mind during the daytime – some idea that he was now able to articulate as sleep approached.

'Daddy,' he said, 'if you want to give me another mother, I want it to be little Marie.'

And without waiting for any answer, he closed his eyes and went to sleep.

Little Marie seemed to pay no attention to the child's strange words other than seeing them as a proof of friendship; she carefully wrapped him up, rekindled the fire, and, as the mist sleeping on the nearby pool seemed in no hurry to thin out, she advised Germain to settle down by the fireside and take a nap.

'I can see you're already falling asleep,' she said, 'since you're not saying a word, and you're gazing into the embers the same way your boy was doing just now. Come on, go to sleep, I'll keep watch over the child and you.'

'*You're* the one that's going to sleep,' replied the ploughman, 'and I'll look after the two of you, as I've never felt less like sleeping; I've got fifty different thoughts buzzing around in my head.'

'Fifty, that's a lot!' said the girl, with a hint of mockery in her voice; 'there are so many people who'd be happy to have just one!'

'Well, if I'm not capable of having fifty, at least I do have one that hasn't left me alone for an hour now.'

'And I can tell you what it is, as well as the ones you were thinking before.'

'Very well! Yes, tell me then, if you can guess it, Marie; you tell me, I'd like to hear it.'

'One hour ago,' she said, 'you were thinking about eating… and just now you were thinking about sleeping.'

'Marie, I'm only an oxherd, but really, you're treating me like an ox! You're a naughty girl, and I can see perfectly well that you don't want to talk to me. So go to sleep, that'll be better than criticising a man who's not feeling very cheerful.'

'If you want to have a talk, let's talk,' said the girl, half reclining next to the boy and leaning her head against the packsaddle. 'You're worrying your head, Germain, and you're not showing much bravery for a man. What would I think of myself if I couldn't fight off my sad thoughts?'

'Yes, of course… and that's just what's bothering me, my poor child! You're going to live far away from your parents and in a horrid land of moors and marshes, where you'll catch autumn fevers, where the wool animals don't thrive, which always worries a shepherdess with good intentions; anyway, you'll be in the midst of strangers who perhaps won't treat you kindly, who won't understand what a good person you are. You know, it pains me more than I can tell you, and I feel just like taking you back to your mother's rather than going on to Fourche.'

'You're speaking very kindly, but not very sensibly, my poor Germain; people shouldn't be cowardly on behalf of their friends, and, instead of showing me the bad side of my fate, you ought to be showing me the good side, as you did when we stopped off for a snack at Mère Rebec's.'

'What do you expect? That's the way it struck me then, and now it strikes me quite differently. You'd do better to find a husband.'

'That's not possible, Germain, I've told you; and as it's not possible, I'm not thinking about it.'

'But what if you *did* find one? Perhaps if you'd tell me what kind of husband you'd like, I'd be able to imagine someone.'

'Imagining isn't the same as finding. I'm not going to imagine anything – there's absolutely no point.'

'You wouldn't be thinking of finding a rich man?'

'No, of course not, since I'm as poor as Job.'

'But if he was comfortably off, it wouldn't hurt you to have a nice house, nice food and nice clothes, and to live in a family of decent folks who'd allow you to look after your mother?'

'Oh if you're going to bring that in, well, yes! Helping my mother, that's all I want.'

'And what if you did find one, even if the man wasn't in the bloom of youth, you wouldn't be too choosy?'

'Ah, you'll have to forgive me, Germain. That's just what I'd have to insist on. I wouldn't like an old man.'

'Not an old man, sure, but what about a man of my age, for example?'

'Your age is old for me, Germain; I'd like someone Bastien's age, even though Bastien's not as good-looking as you are.'

'You'd prefer Bastien the swineherd?' said Germain ill-humouredly. 'A boy with eyes like those of the animals he leads?'

'I'd overlook his eyes because he's only eighteen.'

49

Germain felt horribly jealous.

'So,' he said, 'I can see that you've got a thing for Bastien. That's a funny idea and no mistake!'

'Yes, it would be a funny idea,' replied little Marie, bursting out laughing, 'and he'd make a funny husband. People can get him to believe anything they want. For instance, the other day I'd picked a tomato in our priest's garden; I told him it was a lovely red apple, and he bit into it like a real glutton. You should have seen what a face he pulled! My God, what an ugly mug!'

'So you don't love him, seeing as how you're making fun of him?'

'That wouldn't be much of a reason. But no, I don't love him; he's brutal towards his little sister, and he's not very clean.'

'And you don't feel attracted to anyone else?'

'What's that to you, Germain?'

'It's nothing to me, I'm just making conversation. I can see, my lass, that you've already got some suitor lined up in your head.'

'No, Germain, you're wrong, I don't have anyone yet; someone may come along later: but since I'm not going to get married until I've put a bit of money away, I'm destined to get married late, and to an old man.'

'Well then, take an old man straight away.'

'No! when I'm not young any more, I won't mind either way; right now, it would be different.'

'I can see very well, Marie, that you don't find me attractive; it's all too clear,' said Germain resentfully, and without weighing his words.

Little Marie did not reply. Germain leant over to her – she was asleep; she had fallen, quite overcome by sleep, as if stunned by it, like children who are already asleep even though they continue to babble.

Germain was pleased that she had not paid any attention to his last words; he realised they were not really very sensible, and turned his back on her to take his mind off things and turn his thoughts elsewhere.

But however hard he tried, he could not go to sleep, nor think of anything other than what he had just said. He walked round the fire twenty times, he wandered off, he came back; finally, feeling as agitated as if he had swallowed gunpowder, he leant against the tree that sheltered the two children and gazed at them as they slept.

'I don't know how it was that I'd never realised,' he thought, 'that this little Marie is the prettiest girl in the whole region!... She doesn't have much colour, but her little face is as fresh as a rosebud! What nice lips and a sweet little nose!... She's not very tall for her age, but she's sturdy as a young quail and as light as a finch!... I don't know why people make such a fuss at home about having a big plump woman with a ruddy face... My wife was on the slender and pale side, and I liked her more than anything... This one is rather delicate, but her health is none the worse for that, and she's as pretty as a white kid goat!... And then, what a sweet and honest way she has! You can read how kind-hearted she is from her eyes, even when they are shut tight asleep!... As for intelligence, she's got more of that than my dear Catherine did, you have to admit, and you wouldn't get bored with her... She's cheerful, sensible, hard-working, affectionate and amusing. I can't see what more anyone could wish for...

'But what's the point of my mulling over any of that?' Germain went on, trying to look at things from another angle. 'My father-in-law wouldn't want to hear of it, and the whole family would treat me like a madman!... In any case, she wouldn't want me, the poor child!... She thinks I'm too old – she's told me so... She's not interested, she's hardly worried at the prospect of having more poverty and pain, wearing poor clothes and suffering from hunger for two or three months a year, so long as she can find her heart's content one day, and give herself to a husband she finds attractive... she's right, too! I'd do the same in her place... and right now, if I could follow my own desires, instead of embarking on a marriage that doesn't exactly seem an attractive prospect, I'd choose a girl I really liked...'

The more Germain tried to reason with himself and calm down, the less he could sort it all out. He walked away some twenty paces, losing himself in the mist, and then, suddenly, he found himself kneeling next to the two sleeping children. Once, he even wanted to kiss Petit-Pierre, who'd slipped his arm round Marie's neck, but in the low visibility he made a mistake and Marie, sensing a breath as hot as fire playing on her lips, woke up and gazed at him in alarm, quite unable to understand what was going through his mind.

'I couldn't see you, my poor children!' said Germain, pulling away quickly. 'I almost tripped over you and hurt you.'

Little Marie was innocent enough to believe him, and went back to sleep. Germain moved over to the other side of the fire, and swore to God that he would not budge from it until she had reawoken. He kept his word, but not without a struggle. He thought the effort would drive him mad.

Finally, around midnight, the mist lifted, and Germain could see the stars shining through the trees. The moon also emerged from behind the vapours that covered it and proceeded to scatter diamonds into the damp moss. The trunk of the oak trees remained in a majestic obscurity, but, a little further on, the white stems of the birches resembled a row of phantoms in their shrouds. The fire was reflected in the pool, and the frogs, as they gradually became used to it, hazarded a few reedy and timid notes; the angular branches of the old trees, bristling with pale lichens, stretched out in a criss-cross pattern, like old gaunt arms over the heads of our travellers; it was a fine spot, but so deserted and so melancholy that Germain, tired of the painful thoughts he was enduring there, started to sing and to throw stones into the water to numb the dull throb and frightening ache of solitude. In addition, he wanted to wake up little Marie; and when he saw that she was getting up and looking at the weather, he suggested they set off again.

'In two hours,' he said, 'the approach of day will make the air so cold that we won't be able to bear it, in spite of our fire... Right now, we can see well enough to find our way, and we'll easily come across a house that'll open up to us, or at least some barn where we can spend the rest of the night under cover.'

Marie was not strong-willed; and although she still really felt like sleeping, she got ready to follow Germain.

He picked up his son in his arms without waking him, and told Marie to come and snuggle up in his coat, since she refused to take back her cape that was wrapped around little Pierre.

When he felt the young girl so close to him, Germain, whose spirits had lifted as he forgot his cares for a moment, again started to lose his head. Two or three times he abruptly moved away, and let her walk alone. Then, seeing that she was finding it difficult to follow him, he waited for her, pulled her brusquely over to him, and pressed her so strongly that she was amazed and even annoyed, though she did not dare say so.

Since they did not in the least know from which direction they had set off, they did not know in which one they were heading; as a result, they climbed all the way back through the whole wood, and found themselves, yet again, facing the deserted moorland; they retraced their steps and, after walking this way and that for a good long time, they spotted a glimmer of light through the branches.

'Good! There's a house,' said Germain, 'and some people already awake, since the fire is lit. So it must be quite late?'

But it was not a house – it was the fire of the bivouac they had covered up on leaving; it had rekindled in the breeze…

They had been walking for two hours, only to find themselves back where they had started.

'Well I just about give up!' said Germain, stamping his foot. 'Someone's put a spell on us, that's for sure, and we won't get away from here until daybreak. This spot must be possessed by the Devil.'

'Come on now, don't let's get cross,' said Marie, 'we can cope all right. We'll make a bigger fire, the boy's so well wrapped up he's not in any danger, and spending a night outside isn't going to kill us. Where've you hidden the packsaddle, Germain? Right in the middle of the great holly bush, you great scatterbrain! *Very* easy to get to!'

'Hold the boy, take him so I can pull his bed out of the undergrowth; I don't want you to prick your hands.'

'Done it; here's the bed, and a few pricks aren't exactly sabre wounds,' replied the brave girl.

She again busied herself with putting little Pierre to bed; he was so fast asleep this time that he was quite unaware of this new journey. Germain put so much wood on the fire that the whole forest all around gleamed in its reflected light; but little Marie was at the end of her strength, and though she did not utter a word of complaint, her legs could no longer support her. She was pale and her teeth were chattering with cold and exhaustion. Germain took her in his arms to warm her up; and his anxiety, his compassion, and the promptings of an irresistible tenderness that swept through his heart, all muted his senses. His tongue was loosened as if miraculously, and all his shame fell away.

'Marie,' he said, 'I like you, and I'm really unhappy that you don't like me. If you would accept me as your husband, there wouldn't be a father-in-law, or parents, or neighbours in the world who could stop me giving myself to you. I know that you'd make my children happy, that you'd teach them to respect the memory of their mother, and since I'd be at ease with my conscience, I'd be able to satisfy your heart. I've always had friendly feelings towards you, and just now I feel so much in love that if you asked me to carry out your every wish all my life long, I'd swear that I would, that very minute. Please see how much I love you, and try to forget my age. Because it's a wrong idea people get into their heads when they think a man of thirty is old. And in any case, I'm only twenty-eight! A young girl's frightened of getting criticised if she takes a man who's ten or twelve years older than she is, since it's not the local custom; but I've heard that in other localities, people don't bother about that; quite the opposite, they prefer to give a young thing a proper means of support, a sensible man, of well-tried courage, rather than a young lad who might go off the rails and turn into a bad sort, instead of being the decent chap they'd thought him to be. Anyway, you're only as old as you feel. It depends on your strength and your health. When a man's worn out by too much hard work and poverty or by an immoral lifestyle, he's old by the time he reaches twenty-five. But as for me… But you're not listening, Marie.'

'I am, Germain, I hear you perfectly well,' replied little Marie, 'but I'm remembering what my mother always told me: a woman of sixty is to be pitied when her husband is seventy or seventy-five and can't work any more to feed her. He becomes infirm, and she has to look after him at an age when she herself could really start doing with some comfort and relaxation. That's how people end up destitute.'

'Parents are right to say that, I quite agree, Marie,' replied Germain; 'but then they're prepared to sacrifice the whole time of your youth, which is your best time, to thinking ahead to what will become of you at an age when you're no longer good for anything, and where it's all the same whether you end up this way or that way. But *I'm* not in any danger of starving to death in my old age. I even have every prospect of putting something away, since, living with my wife's parents, I work a lot and spend nothing. Anyway, I'll love you so much, you see, that it will stop me growing old. They say that when a man's happy, he doesn't age, and I feel that I'm younger than Bastien, loving you the way I do; after all, *he* doesn't love you, he's too stupid, too childish to understand how pretty and kind you are, and how likely you are to have many suitors. Come on, Marie, don't hate me, I'm not a bad fellow: I made my Catherine happy, she said on her deathbed, before God, that I'd brought her real contentment, and she recommended that I get remarried. It seems as if her spirit spoke to her son this evening, as he went off to sleep. Didn't you hear what he said? And how his little lips were trembling, while his eyes looked into thin air, seeing something that we couldn't see! He could see his mother, you can rest assured, and it was she who was making him say that he wanted you to replace her.'

'Germain,' replied Marie, astonished and pensive, 'you are speaking sincerely and everything you say is true. I'm sure I would do well to love you, if that didn't put your parents out too much: but what do you expect of me? I just don't have those feelings for you in my heart. I'm very fond of you, but although your age doesn't make you seem unattractive to me, it does frighten me. It seems to me that you *are* something to me, something like an uncle or a godfather; so I owe you respect, and there'd be times when you'd treat me as a little girl rather than as your wife and equal. And then, my friends would maybe make fun of me, and although it's silly to pay any attention to that, I think I'd be ashamed and a bit sad on our wedding day.'

'Those are childish reasons; you're talking just like a child, Marie!'

'Well, yes, I *am* a child,' she said, 'and that's why I'm nervous of a man who's too sensible. You can see perfectly well that I'm too young for you, since you're already telling me off for not speaking very sensibly! I can't be any more sensible than my age.'

'Ah my God, how pitiful I am! I'm so clumsy, I can't even put what I think into words!' cried Germain. 'Marie, you don't love me, that's the nub of it; you find me too simple and too boorish. If you did love me a bit, you wouldn't see my failings so clearly. But you don't love me – and that's that!'

'Well, it's not my fault,' she replied, a little wounded that he had stopped calling her *tu*; 'I'm doing everything I can by hearing you out, but the more I try, the less I can get it into my head that we ought to be husband and wife.'

Germain did not reply. He put his head in his hands, and little Marie could not make out whether he was crying, sulking or had gone to sleep. She was a little worried to see him so glum, and not to be able to guess what was going on in his mind; but she did not dare speak to him any more, and since she was too astonished at what had just happened for her to feel like going back to sleep, she awaited the day with impatience, continuing to tend the fire and watch over the child, about whom Germain seemed to have quite forgotten. However, Germain was not sleeping; he was not brooding over his fate, nor was he hatching any bold projects or laying any plans for seduction. He was suffering – a whole mountain of sorrow was weighing down on his heart. He wished he were dead. Everything seemed to have gone wrong for him, and if he had been able to cry, he would have cried bucketfuls. But he was angry with himself in his pain, and he could hardly breathe, unable and unwilling as he was to complain.

When day had dawned and the noises of the countryside announced this to Germain, he raised his face from his hands and got up. He saw that little Marie had not slept either, but he could not think of anything to say to her that would express his solicitude. He had quite lost heart. He again hid Grey's packsaddle in the bushes, slung his bag across his shoulders, and, holding his son by the hand, said:

'Well, Marie, right now we're going to try and finish our journey. Do you want me to take you to Les Ormeaux?'

'We can leave the wood together,' she replied, 'and when we've worked out where we are, we can go our separate ways.'

Germain did not reply. He was wounded that the young girl had not asked him to take her as far as Les Ormeaux, and he did not realise that he had offered to do so in a tone of voice that seemed calculated to provoke a refusal.

A woodcutter they met a couple of hundred paces further on put them on the right road, and told them that once they had passed the big meadow they merely needed to turn right and left respectively, to reach their different lodgings, which in any case were so close together that you could distinctly see the houses of Fourche from the farm at Les Ormeaux, and vice versa.

Then, when they had thanked the woodcutter and were just leaving him behind, the latter called them back to ask them if they had not lost a horse.

'I found,' he told them, 'a fine grey mare in my yard, or perhaps the wolf forced her to seek refuge there. My dogs were yapping all night long, and at daybreak I saw our friend horse in my shed – where she still is. Go and have a look; if you recognise her, take her with you.'

As Germain had already given him a description of Grey and convinced himself it was indeed her, he set off to find his packsaddle. So little Marie offered to take his son to Les Ormeaux, where he would come and pick him up when he'd announced his arrival at Fourche.

'He's a bit dirty after the night we've just spent,' she said. 'I'll clean his clothes, I'll give his sweet little face a wash, and comb his hair, and when he's all spruce and handsome, you'll be able to present him to your new family.'

'And who's told you I want to go to Fourche?' replied Germain ill-humouredly. 'Perhaps I won't go!'

'Oh, but yes, Germain, you must go, you will go,' replied the young girl.

'You're in a real hurry to see me marry another woman, so as to be sure I won't bother you any more?'

'Oh come on, Germain, stop thinking about that – it's just an idea you got into your head during the night because that spot of bad luck had turned your wits a bit. But right now you need to start being sensible again; I promise that I'll forget what you told me and never mention it to anyone.'

'Oh, you can tell them if you want. I'm not in the habit of denying anything I've said. What I told you was true, sincere, and I don't need to blush for it in front of anyone.'

'Yes, but if your wife knew that at the very moment you were arriving, you'd been thinking about another woman, it might make her rather ill-disposed towards you. So pay attention to the words you say now; don't look at me like that in front of everybody, with such an odd expression. Remember Père Maurice who's counting on your obedience – he'd be really angry with me if I distracted you from doing his bidding. Goodbye, Germain; I'm taking Petit-Pierre with me so as to force you to go to Fourche. He's a pledge that I'm keeping for you.'

'So do you want to go with her?' said the ploughman to his son, seeing that he was clinging to Marie's hand and would resolutely follow her.

'Yes, Father,' replied the child, who had followed and understood in his own way what they had quite openly been saying in front of him. 'I'm going off with my darling little Marie; you can come and fetch me when you've finished getting married, but I want Marie still to be my little mother.'

'You see – *he* wants it!' said Germain to the young girl. 'Listen, Petit-Pierre,' he added, 'I want her to be your mother and stay with you always; she's the one who doesn't want to. Try and get her to grant to you what she's refusing to me.'

'Don't worry, Father, I'll make her say yes; little Marie always does what I want.'

He went off with the young girl. Germain was left alone, sadder and more irresolute than ever.

All the same, when he had smartened up his clothes and his horse's tack, in disarray from the journey, climbed back onto Grey and asked someone to point him in the right direction, he reflected that there was no going back, and that he would have to forget this unsettled night as if it were a dangerous dream.

He found Père Léonard on the threshold of his white house, sitting on a fine wooden bench painted spinach-green. There were six stone steps leading up to the front door, which showed that the house had a cellar. The wall round the garden and the hemp field was pebble-dashed. It was a fine place, and could easily have been taken for a middle-class residence.

The future father-in-law came up to meet Germain and, after five minutes spent asking him how his whole family was, he added the time-hallowed phrase that people use when they wish politely to question someone they have met about the purpose of their journey:

'*So, you're just passing through then, are you?*'

'I've come to see you,' replied the ploughman, 'and to bring you this small gift of game from my father-in-law, and tell you, also on his behalf, that you'll already know what it is that's brought me to your place.'

'Ha! Ha!' said Père Léonard, laughing and patting himself on his round belly, 'I see, I understand, I get it!'

And, with a wink, he added:

'You won't be the first to be presenting your compliments, my young fellow. There are already three chaps at home, all waiting like you. *I'm* not going to send anyone away, and I'd be hard put to say yes or no to anyone, since they're all good matches. Still, thanks to Père Maurice and the fine quality of the land you cultivate, I'd prefer it to be you. But my daughter is an adult and can dispose of her own property, so she'll act as she sees fit. Come in, introduce yourself; I hope you've drawn the lucky number!'

'Oh, excuse me, I'm sorry,' replied Germain, completely taken aback to discover he was a supernumerary where he had been expecting to be the only one. 'I didn't know your daughter was already handsomely provided for with suitors, and I hadn't come to compete for her with others.'

'If you thought, just because you kept her waiting,' replied Père Maurice, without losing his good humour, 'that my daughter had been left without a suitor, you were gravely mistaken, my lad. Catherine has what it takes to attract men with marriage on their minds, and she'll have all too many to choose from. But come on now, come into the house, don't lose heart. She's a woman worth fighting for.'

And pushing Germain by the shoulders, he exclaimed, with rough merriment, as he entered the house:

'I say, Catherine, here's one more for you!'

This jovial but coarse way of being introduced to the widow, in the presence of her other suitors, was the final straw for the ploughman, who was perplexed and quite put out. He felt gauche and stood there for a while, not daring to lift his eyes to look at the beauty and her court.

Widow Guérin was a fine figure of a woman and not without a certain youthful freshness. But the expression on her face and the clothes she was wearing immediately struck Germain as disagreeable. She had a bold, self-satisfied demeanour, and her wimples adorned with three rows of lace, her silk apron and her black nankeen lace shawl hardly fitted the picture he had of a serious, orderly widow. Her rather showy clothes and casual manners made her seem old and ugly to him, even though she was neither of these things. He reflected that her pretty outfit and playful manners would suit someone of the age and perceptiveness of little Marie, but that this widow had a heavy-handed, rather hit-and-miss sense of humour, and that she was wearing her finery without much distinction.

The three suitors were sitting at a table laden with wine and meat, set out there for them all Sunday morning long – Père Léonard enjoyed showing off his wealth, and the widow was not averse to putting her fine cutlery on display and keeping a well-furnished table like a woman of property. Germain, simple and trusting as he was, observed all this with some astuteness, and for the first time in his life he stayed on the defensive when clinking glasses. Père Léonard had forced him to take his place with his rivals, and, sitting down opposite him, he lavished his attentions on him, and took the very best care of his comfort. The gift of

61

game, despite the inroads Germain had made on it to assuage his own hunger, was still copious enough to create an effect. The widow seemed impressed, and the suitors glanced at it disdainfully.

Germain felt ill at ease in this company and ate only reluctantly. Père Léonard teased him.

'You're looking down in the dumps,' he said, 'and you've hardly touched your glass. You mustn't let love put you off your food and drink – a lover boy who goes without can't think of nice things to say the way a man can when he's brightened up his ideas with a drop or two of wine.'

Germain was mortified to think they assumed he was already in love, and the widow's affected mannerisms – lowering her eyes and smiling, like someone who thinks she's got it all in the bag – made him feel like protesting against what they took as her victory over him; but he was afraid of seeming uncivil, so he smiled and stuck it out.

The widow's wooers struck him as three complete boors. They must have been fairly rich for her to give their suit a hearing. The one was over forty, and almost as fat as Père Léonard; another was blind in one eye and drank so much it left him completely sozzled; the third was young, quite a handsome lad, but he kept trying to be witty and his inane remarks fell so flat that you felt sorry for him. Still, the widow laughed at them as much as if she had admired all his silly jokes – and this hardly showed much taste on her part. Germain at first thought that she was infatuated with him; but he soon realised that he himself was being egged on in a particular way, and that they wanted him to be more communicative. This merely gave him a reason for feeling and seeming cold and serious.

Then it was time to go to Mass, and everyone rose from table to make their way there together. They had to go to Mers, a good half-league from there, and Germain was so tired that he could really have done with taking time for a nap beforehand; but he was not in the habit of missing Mass, and he set off with the others.

There were many people on the road, and the widow stepped out proudly, escorted by her three suitors, giving her arm to each of them in turn, swelled with conceit and holding her head high. She would really have loved to show off the fourth suitor to the passers-by; but Germain found it so ridiculous to be seen running along after her petticoats, in front of everyone, that he kept himself decently aloof, chatting to Père Léonard, and finding a way of keeping him busy talking so that they would not seem to be part of the group.

When they reached the village, the widow waited for them to catch up. She absolutely wanted to make her entrance with all her court around her; but Germain, refusing her this satisfaction, left Père Léonard, went to say hello to several people he knew, and entered the church through another door. The widow was piqued at this.

After the Mass, she displayed herself in all her triumph on the lawn where they were dancing, and she opened the dance with her three swains in succession. Germain watched her, and decided that she danced well, but rather affectedly.

'Well then!' said Léonard, patting him on the shoulder, 'aren't you going to ask my daughter for a dance? You're much too shy!'

'I've stopped dancing since I lost my wife,' replied the ploughman.

'Well, since you've started looking for another one, you can lay aside mourning in your heart, just as you have in your clothes.'

'That's not a reason, Père Léonard; anyway, I feel too old, and I don't like dancing any more.'

'Listen,' said Père Léonard, drawing him aside to a place where they could be alone, 'you felt put out when you arrived at mine and saw the place already besieged on all sides, and I can see that you're a proud fellow; but you're hardly being very sensible, my lad. My daughter is used to being courted, especially over the last two years, ever since her mourning period was over, and it's not for her to come bowing and scraping to you.'

'Your daughter's been on the marriage market for two years already, and she still hasn't made her mind up?' said Germain.

'She doesn't want to rush things, and she's right. Though she looks forward and may strike you as not very thoughtful, in fact she's a very sensible woman, and knows exactly what she's doing.'

'I don't think she does,' said Germain innocently. 'She's got three suitors on her tail, and if she did know what she wanted, there'd be at least two of them she would find superfluous and would ask to stay at home.'

'Really? Why? You just don't get it, Germain. She doesn't want the old one, nor the one who's blind in one eye, nor the youngster, I'm almost sure of it, but if she sent them all packing, everyone would think she wanted to stay a widow, and nobody else would come.'

'Ah, I see – those ones are like a shop sign!'

'As you say. What's wrong with that, if it suits them?'[4]

'Each to his own!' said Germain.

'I can see it wouldn't be to yours. But listen, we could come to some agreement, supposing you were to be preferred: we could leave the coast clear for you.'

'Yes, supposing! And while I wait to find out, how long would I need to stand around sniffing the wind?'

'That depends on you, I think, if you can say the right things and win her over. Up until now my daughter has realised very clearly that the best time of her life would be while she was letting herself be courted, and she doesn't feel in much of a hurry to become a man's servant, when she can command several of them all at once. And so, as long as she enjoys the game, she can have a good time; but if she starts to like you more than the game, the game can stop. You simply need not to be put off. Come back every Sunday, ask her for a dance, make it clear you've joined the lists, and if you seem nicer and more well bred than the others, one fine day you'll be told as much.'

'Excuse me, Père Léonard, your daughter has the right to act however she wants, and I don't have any right to criticise her. In her place, I must say I'd behave differently; I'd be more frank about it all, and I wouldn't waste the time of men who I'm sure have better things to do than prowl round a woman who doesn't give a damn about them. But anyway, if that's what amuses her and keeps her happy, it's none of my business. Still, there is one thing I really need to tell you, something that I've been a bit too embarrassed to admit to you since this morning, seeing as you started off getting my intentions wrong, and didn't give me any time to reply. And as a result, you think something is true that isn't. So what you need to know is that I didn't come here with the aim of asking for your daughter's hand in marriage, but to buy a yoke of oxen from you, the ones you're intending to take to the fair next week. My father-in-law's got the idea they'd just do for him.'

'I understand, Germain,' replied Léonard placidly. 'You changed your mind when your saw my daughter with her lovers. Whatever you wish. It seems that what attracts some people puts other people off, and you have every right to withdraw since, after all, you hadn't yet stated your intentions. If you really do want to buy my oxen, come and see them in their pasture; we can have a talk about it, and whether we strike the deal or not, you can come and have dinner with us before you go back.'

'I don't want you to put yourself out,' replied Germain, 'maybe you've got things to do here. But I'm getting a bit bored of watching the dancing and doing nothing. I'll go and have a look at your animals, and I'll see you at your place later.'

With these words, Germain slipped away and headed off towards the meadows, where Léonard had as a matter of fact pointed out part of his herd of livestock in the distance. It was quite true that Père Maurice wanted to buy some, and Germain reflected that if he brought a fine yoke of oxen back, at a moderate price, he would more easily be forgiven for having deliberately neglected to carry out the purpose of his journey.

He walked quickly and soon found himself only a short distance away from Les Ormeaux. Then he felt like going to give his son a hug, and even seeing little Marie again, although he had lost any hope and driven away the thought of gaining his happiness from her. Everything he had just seen and heard – that flirtatious, proud woman, that father both sly and limited in intelligence, who encouraged his daughter in her habits of pride and insincerity, that luxury typical of towns that seemed to him an infraction of the dignity of rural ways, that time wasted in silly, meaningless words, that home that was so different from his own, and above all that profound sense of unease that the man of the fields experiences when he takes time away from his hard-working habits – all the boredom and confusion he had endured over the past few hours gave Germain a longing to be back with his son and the girl from next door. Even if he had not been in love with her, he would still have sought her out to take his mind off things and regain his usual calm and tranquil frame of mind.

But he looked in vain through the meadows all around; he could find neither little Marie nor little Pierre, and yet it was the time of day when the shepherds are in the fields. There was a great herd in a pen; he asked a young lad who was guarding them whether they were the sheep from the farm at Les Ormeaux.

'Yes,' said the child.

'Are you their shepherd? Do boys look after the woolly-coated animals from the farms in your district?'

'No. I'm looking after them today because the shepherdess has gone away – she was poorly.'

'But haven't you got a new shepherdess, the one who arrived this morning?'

'Oh, yes… but she's gone away too.'

'Gone away? Didn't she have a child with her?'

'Yes: a little boy who was crying. They both headed off after a couple of hours.'

'Headed off? Where?'

'Back where they'd come from, apparently. I didn't ask them.'

'But why were they going?' asked Germain, feeling more and more worried.

'Strewth, how should I know?'

'Couldn't they agree about the wages? But it must all have been arranged in advance.'

'I really can't say. I saw them going in and coming out, that's all.'

Germain went over to the farm and questioned the tenant farmers. No one could give him any explanations; the only certain thing to emerge was that, after talking with the farmer, the young girl had left without saying a word, taking the crying child with her.

'Did they maltreat my son?' exclaimed Germain, his eyes flaring.

'You mean that was your son? So what was he doing with that little girl? And where do you come from – what's your name?'

Germain could see that, as was the custom in this part of the world, they would reply to his questions with yet more questions; he stamped with impatience and asked to speak to the master.

The master was not there; he did not usually stay for the whole day when he came to the farm. He had got onto his horse and ridden off to another of his farms, they did not know which one.

'But look,' said Germain, in prey to intense anxiety, 'do you really not know why the girl would have left?'

The tenant farmer exchanged a strange smile with his wife, and then replied that he knew nothing about it, and it was none of his business. All that Germain could discover was that the young girl and the child had set off for Fourche. He rushed over to Fourche; the widow and her suitors were not yet back, and neither was Père Léonard. The servant woman told him that a young girl and a child had come asking for him, but since she didn't know them, she had not wanted to let them in, and had told them to go to Mers.

'And why did you refuse to let them in?' said Germain angrily. 'Are you all so mistrustful in these parts that you won't open your doors to your neighbours?'

'Heavens above!' replied the servant, 'in a rich house like this one, there's every reason to be on our guard. I'm responsible for everything when the masters are away, and I can't open up to just anyone.'

'That's a horrid custom,' said Germain, 'and I'd rather be poor than live in fear like that. Goodbye, miss! Goodbye to your nasty little region!'

He made enquiries at the nearby houses. They had seen the shepherdess and the child. Since the boy had left Belair unexpectedly, without being spruced up, his smock a bit torn and his little lambskin jerkin on his body, and since, too, little Marie was, with good reason, quite poorly dressed at all times, they had been taken for beggars. They'd been offered some bread; the girl had accepted a piece for the boy, who was hungry, then she had quickly left, and reached the woods.

Germain thought for a few moments, then he asked if the farmer at Les Ormeaux had not come to Fourche.

'Yes,' they replied; 'he rode by a few moments after the girl.'

'Was he chasing after her?'

'Ah, so you know him, then?' said the local innkeeper, to whom Germain had addressed his question. 'He was that; he's a devil of a fellow for chasing after the girls. But I don't think he managed to catch that one, though after all, if once he'd seen her...'

'That's enough. Thank you!'

And he flew rather than ran to Léonard's stable. He flung the packsaddle over Grey, jumped onto her, and set off at a gallop in the direction of the Chanteloube woods.

His heart was pounding with anxiety and anger; sweat was pouring down his face. He spurred Grey on until he drew blood, but finding herself on the way home to her stable, she did not need any urging to get a move on.

14
The Old Woman

Germain was soon back at the place where he had spent the night by the side of the pool. The fire was still smoking; an old woman was picking up what was left of the stock of dead wood that little Marie had piled up there. Germain halted to question her. She was deaf and, misunderstanding his intentions, she said:

'Yes, my boy, this is the Devil's Pool. It's a bad spot, and you mustn't come close to it without throwing three stones into it out of your left hand, while making the sign of the cross with your right – that drives the spirits away. Otherwise terrible things happen to people who walk round it.'

'That's not what I'm talking about!' replied Germain, going up to her and shouting his head off. 'Didn't you see a girl and a child going into the woods?'

'Yes,' said the old woman, 'a little boy got drowned here!'

Germain shuddered from head to foot; but fortunately the old woman added:

'It all happened a long time ago; in memory of the accident, they'd planted a fine cross there, but one night when there was a really big storm, the evil spirits threw it into the water. You can still see part of it. If anyone was so unfortunate as to stop here at night, he'd be sure of not being able to get out again before daylight. He could walk and walk, he could travel two hundred leagues through the wood – he'd still keep coming back to the same place.'

The ploughman's imagination was struck, in spite of himself, by what he heard, and the idea of the terrible thing that would happen and thereby completely justify the old woman's assertions took hold of his mind so rapidly that he broke out into a cold sweat all over. Giving up any hope of getting any more information, he leapt back onto his horse and again started riding up and down through the wood, calling for Pierre with all his strength, and whistling, cracking his whip and breaking the branches so as to fill the forest with the sound of his progress, then listening to hear if any voice replied; but all he heard was the bells of the cows scattered through the undergrowth, and the savage squeals of the pigs fighting over the acorns.

Finally Germain heard behind him the noise of a horse following his tracks, and a middle-aged man, brown-complexioned, robust and quite well dressed, shouted to him to stop. Germain had never seen the farmer from Les Ormeaux; but in his rage he felt instinctively that this was indeed the man. He turned round, and, measuring him with his glance, waited to hear what he would have to say to him.

'You haven't seen a young girl of fifteen or sixteen passing this way, with a little boy?' said the farmer, affecting an air of indifference, although he was visibly overwrought.

'And what do you want from her?' replied Germain, not even trying to disguise his anger.

'I could very well tell you it's none of your business, my friend! But since I don't have any reason to conceal it, I can tell you that she's a shepherdess I'd hired for the year without knowing her... When I saw her arriving, she seemed to me to be too young and not strong enough for farm work. I thanked her, but I wanted to give her a little something in return for her journey, and she went off in a huff while my back was turned... She was in such a hurry that she even forgot a few of her things and her purse, not that there's much in it, that's for sure – just a few coppers probably!... but as I had to come this way anyhow, I thought I might meet her and give her back what she'd left behind, and what I owe her.'

Germain was too decent a man not to hesitate when he heard this story which, if not altogether plausible, was at least possible. He fixed a piercing stare on the farmer, who outfaced this scrutiny with a great deal of impudence or innocence.

'I want to get to the bottom of this,' Germain said to himself.

And, mastering his indignation, he said:

'She's a girl from back home – I know her; she must be somewhere round here... Let's keep going together... I'm sure we'll find her.'

'You're right,' said the farmer. 'Let's keep going... though if we don't meet her at the end of the path, I'm giving up... I need to head off on the Ardentes road.'

'Oh!' thought the ploughman, 'I'm not leaving you! Even if it means riding round and round the Devil's Pool with you for twenty-four hours! Wait!' said Germain suddenly, gazing at a clump of broom that

71

was waving about strangely. 'Hey! Hey there! Petit-Pierre, is that you, son?'

The boy, recognising his father's voice, emerged from the broom, hopping and skipping like a roebuck, but when he saw that Germain was with the farmer, he halted, as if in fear, and stood there looking irresolute.

'Come here, Pierre! Come on, it's me!' cried the ploughman, galloping up to him, and jumping down from his horse to pick him up in his arms. 'And where's little Marie?'

'She's there, hiding, because she's frightened of that nasty black man, and so am I.'

'Oh, don't worry! I'm here now... Marie! Marie! It's me!'

Marie crawled out, and as soon as she saw Germain, with the farmer close behind him, she ran over and threw herself into his arms, and clinging to him like a daughter to her father, she said:

'Ah, Germain, you're a brave man, you'll defend me; I'm not afraid with you.'

Germain shuddered. He gazed at Marie; she was pale, her clothes were torn by the thorns she had run through, trying to reach the thickets, like a doe with hunters in hot pursuit. But there was neither shame nor despair in her face.

'Your master wants to talk to you,' he told her, closely observing her expression.

'My master?' she said, with pride in her voice; '*that* man isn't my master and never will be!... *You're* my master, Germain. I want you to take me back with you... I'll serve you for free!'

The farmer had come forward, feigning a certain impatience.

'Hey now, my lass,' he said, 'you left something at our place and I'm bringing it back for you.'

'Oh no, sir,' replied little Marie, 'I didn't leave anything, and I don't have anything to ask of you...'

'Just you listen,' replied the farmer, '*I've* got something to say to you!... Come on now!... Don't be afraid... just a couple of words...'

'You can say them in front of everyone... I don't have any secrets with you.'

'Come and take your money, at least.'

'My money? You don't owe me anything, thank God!'

'Just as I thought,' muttered Germain to himself. 'But never mind that, Marie… listen to what he has to say to you… I'm curious to hear it myself. You can tell me afterwards; I have my own reasons. Go up to his horse… I'm not letting you out of my sight.'

Marie took three steps towards the farmer, who leant over the pummel of his saddle, and said to her, lowering his voice:

'Look, my lass, here's a fine louis d'or for you! You won't breathe a word, do you hear? I'll say I found you weren't strong enough to work on my farm… And let's say no more about it… I'll call by at yours one of these days, and if you haven't breathed a word to anyone, I'll give you something else… And then, if you decide to be more sensible, you only have to say. I'll bring you back to mine, or I'll come and have a chat with you, at dusk in the fields. What would you like me to bring you as a present?'

'This is *my* present to *you*, sir!' replied Marie aloud, flinging his louis d'or back in his face, pretty roughly, too. 'Accept my thanks, and I'll just ask you kindly, next time you're passing our way, to please give me advance warning – all the boys in my neighbourhood will come out to meet you, 'cos where we live, they're very fond of gentlemen who try to sweet-talk poor girls! You'll see; they'll be waiting for you.'

'You're a liar and you're talking a load of nonsense!' said the enraged farmer, raising his stick menacingly. 'You'd like people to believe that something happened when it didn't, but you won't get any money out of me – everyone knows your sort!'

Marie had retreated in alarm, but Germain had sprung forward to the bridle of the farmer's horse and said, shaking it violently:

'Now it's all clear! We have a pretty good idea what all this is about… Down you get, my lad, down you get! Let's the two of us have a little chat about this!'

The farmer was in no hurry to accept the challenge; he spurred on his horse to free himself, and tried to lash out at the ploughman's hands with his stick to force him to let go, but Germain dodged the blow and, seizing him by the leg, he threw him and made him topple onto the bracken, where he knocked him to the ground, even though the farmer had managed to get back to his feet and was defending himself quite vigorously. Once Germain was standing over him, he said:

'You coward! I could give you a real thrashing if I wanted to! But I don't like doing wrong, and anyway, nothing I did to punish you would make you mend your ways... Still, you're not moving from here until you've asked that young girl on your knees to forgive you.'

The farmer, who was well acquainted with this kind of situation, tried to pass it off with a laugh. He claimed his sin had not been all that serious, since it consisted in no more than words, and that he was quite ready to ask for forgiveness, on condition he could give the girl a hug, and they all went to drink a tankard of beer at the nearest inn, and parted on the best of terms.

'You make me sick!' replied Germain, pushing his face into the ground, 'and I can't wait till I've seen the last of your ugly mug. Go on, blush if you can, and try to take the path of the shamefaced when you do come our way.'*

He picked up the farmer's stick of holly, broke it across his knees to demonstrate what strong wrists he had, and hurled the fragments away with contempt.

Then, taking his son in one hand, and little Marie in the other, he headed off, trembling all over with indignation.

* This is the path that leads away from the main road at the entry to villages and skirts round them. The idea is that shamefaced people, afraid of receiving some well-merited insult, take it to avoid being seen. [Note by G. Sand.]

Within a quarter of an hour they had crossed the heathland. They were trotting along the high road, and Grey was whinnying at everything she saw and recognised. Petit-Pierre was telling his father as much as he had understood about what had happened.

'When we arrived,' he said, '*that man* came to talk to *my Marie* in the sheep barn where we went straight away, to see the fine sheep. I'd climbed into the manger to play, and *that man* couldn't see me. Then he said hello to my Marie, and he kissed her.'

'You let him kiss you, Marie?' said Germain, trembling with rage.

'I thought he was just being polite, I thought it was the way they greet newcomers in these parts, like in yours the way Grandmother kisses the young girls who enter her service, to show them that she's adopting them and that she will be like a mother to them.'

'And then,' said Petit-Pierre, who was proud that he had an adventure to relate, '*that man* said something nasty to you, something that you told me never to repeat and not to remember, so I forgot it straight away. But if my father wants me to tell him what it was…'

'No, my Pierre, I don't want to hear, and I don't want you ever to remember it.'

'In that case, I'll forget it again,' continued the child. 'And then, *that man* seemed to get cross because Marie told him that she was leaving. He told her that he'd give her whatever she wanted, a hundred francs! And my Marie got cross too. Then he came up to her as if he wanted to hurt her. I was frightened, and I threw myself against Marie and started shouting. Then *that man* said, he said, "What the…? Where's this kid come from? Throw him out!" And he lifted his stick to beat me. But my Marie stopped him, and she said to him, she said, "We'll talk later, sir; right now I need to take this boy to Fourche, and then I'll come back." And as soon as he'd gone out of the sheep barn, my Marie said to me, she said, "Let's run for it, Pierre, let's get out of here as fast as we can – he's a wicked man, and he'll only hurt us if we stay." Then we slipped along behind the barns, we crossed a little meadow, and we went over to Fourche looking for you. But you weren't there and they wouldn't let us wait for you. And then that man, who'd got onto his horse, came up behind us, and we ran on ahead, and then we came to hide in the wood. And then he came along too, and when we heard him coming, we hid. And then, when he'd gone by, we started running again to get back home; and in the end you came along and found us; and that's how it all happened. Aren't I right, Marie, I haven't forgotten anything?'

'No, Pierre, and what you've said is all true. And now, Germain, you can be my witness and you can tell everyone back home that if I wasn't able to stay there, it wasn't because I was lazy or didn't want to work.'

'And you, now, Marie,' said Germain, 'let me put this to you: just ask yourself if, when it's a question of defending a woman and punishing insolence, a man of twenty-eight is really too old? I'd just like to know if Bastien, or any other handsome young lad lucky enough to be ten years younger than me, wouldn't have been flattened by *that man*, as Petit-Pierre calls him – what do you think?'

'I think, Germain, that you have done me a great favour, and I'll thank you all my life long.'

'That's it?'

'Daddy,' said the boy, 'I forgot to tell little Marie what I'd promised you. I didn't have time, but I'll tell her when we get home, and I'll tell Grandmother too.'

His son's promise finally made Germain think. Now he would have to explain the situation to his parents and, by setting out his grievances against Widow Guérin, to conceal from them what other ideas had predisposed him to so much sharpness and severity towards her. When you are happy and proud, plucking up the courage to get others to accept your happiness seems easy enough, but being turned down on the one side and rebuked on the other does not make for a very pleasant situation.

Fortunately, little Pierre was asleep when they arrived back at the farm, and Germain put him down, without waking him, on his bed. Then he started going into all the reasons he could give for what had happened. Père Maurice, sitting on his three-legged stool, at the entrance to the house, listened gravely, and though he was displeased at the result of the trip, when Germain described the way the widow was resorting to systematic flirtation and asked his father-in-law whether he,

Germain, had time to go over there to court her fifty-two Sundays in the year, at the risk of being turned down at the end of the twelve months, his father-in-law replied, bowing his head in agreement:

'You're not wrong, Germain; you couldn't have done that.'

And then, when Germain related how he had been forced to bring back little Marie as quickly as possible to protect her from the insults and perhaps the violence of an unworthy master, Père Maurice again nodded his agreement, saying:

'You weren't wrong, Germain; you had to do it.'

When Germain had finished his story and explained his reasons, his father-in-law and mother-in-law simultaneously heaved a great sigh of resignation as they gazed at one another. Then the head of the family rose to his feet, saying:

'Well, may God's will be done! Either you get on well with someone, or you don't!'

'Come and have supper, Germain,' said his mother-in-law. 'It's a pity it didn't turn out better, but anyway, it seems that it wasn't God's will. We'll have to look elsewhere.'

'Yes,' added the old man, 'as my wife says, we'll look elsewhere.'

There was no further noise in the house, and when, the next day, little Pierre rose with the larks, at daybreak, since he no longer had the excitement of the extraordinary events of the preceding days, he relapsed into the apathy of the peasant boys of his age, forgot everything that had trotted through his head, and concentrated on playing with his brothers and *playing grown-ups* with the oxen and horses.

Germain tried to forget it too, by immersing himself once more in work; but he became so depressed and preoccupied that everyone noticed. He did not speak to little Marie, he did not even look at her; and yet, if anyone had asked him in what meadow she was and which path she had taken, there was not a single hour in the day when he would not have been able to give the right reply – if he had wanted to reply. He had not dared to ask his parents to take her in at the farm for the winter, and yet he knew perfectly well that she must be suffering from poverty. But she was not, and Mère Guillette was never able to understand how it was that her little stock of wood never went down, and her shed was full in the morning when she had left it almost empty the evening before. It was the same with the wheat and the potatoes. Someone was coming through the skylight of the granary and emptying a bag onto the floor without waking anyone and without leaving any traces. The old woman was both worried and delighted at this; she swore her daughter to silence, saying that if anyone came to know of the miracle that was happening at her home, they would think she was a witch. She did indeed think that the Devil was involved, but she was in no great hurry to fall out with him by bringing down the priest's exorcisms on her house; she told herself that there would be time for that when Satan came to ask for her soul in return for his favours.

Little Marie understood the truth of the situation more clearly, but she did not dare speak of it to Germain, for fear of seeing him harping on about his idea of marriage again, and she pretended not to notice anything when she was with him.

One day, Mère Maurice happened to be alone with Germain in the orchard, and she said to him amicably:

'My poor son-in-law, I don't think you're very well. You're not eating as well as you usually do, you don't laugh any more, you're less and less talkative. Has someone in our household, or one of us, accidentally offended you?'

'No, Mother,' replied Germain, 'you have always been as kind to me as the mother who brought me into the world, and I'd be really ungrateful if I complained about you, or your husband, or anyone in your household.'

'In that case, my child, it's your sadness over the death of your wife that's hanging over you again. Instead of disappearing with time, your gloom is getting worse, and you really must do what your father-in-law quite sensibly told you to do: you must get remarried.'

'Yes, Mother, that's what I think too; but the women whom you advised me to seek out don't suit me. When I see them, instead of forgetting my Catherine, I think all the more of her.'

'It seems, Germain, that we haven't judged your taste in women correctly. So you must help us out by telling us the truth. There really must be a woman who's made for you somewhere, since the good Lord doesn't create a single person without ensuring they can find happiness in another person. So if you know where to find that woman you need, then take her, and whether she's beautiful or ugly, young or old, rich or poor, we've made up our minds, my old man and me, to give you our consent; we're tired of seeing you so depressed, and we can't have any peace of mind unless you do too.'

'Mother, you're as kind as the good Lord, and my father too,' replied Germain; 'but your compassion isn't enough to remedy my gloom: the girl I'd like doesn't want me.'

'That must be because she's too young? It's crazy for you to get attached to a slip of a thing.'

'Well, yes, Mother dear, I *am* crazy enough to have got attached to a slip of a thing, and I'm not pleased with myself. I'm doing the very best

I can not to think of her any more; but whether I'm working or resting, whether I'm at Mass or in my bed, with my children or with you, I'm always thinking of her, and I just can't think of anything else.'

'So it's like a spell someone's put on you, Germain? There's only one remedy for that – the girl in question must change her mind and listen to you. So I'll have to get involved myself, and see if it's possible. You can tell me where she lives and what her name is.'

'Oh but, Mother dear, I daren't!' said Germain, 'since you'll make fun of me.'

'I won't make fun of you, Germain – you're really unhappy, and I don't want to make you any unhappier. Is it Fanchette, by any chance?'

'No, Mother, not her.'

'Or Rosette?'

'No.'

'Do tell me then, otherwise I'll never get to the end if I have to name all the girls in the land.'

Germain lowered his head and could not bring himself to reply.

'All right!' said Mère Maurice, 'I'll leave you alone for today, Germain; perhaps tomorrow you'll be able to confide a bit more in me, or your sister-in-law will be smarter at questioning you.'

And she picked up her basket to go and hang out her laundry on the bushes.

Germain did what children do when they make up their minds to tell the truth, realising that at least that way people will not bother them any more. He followed his mother-in-law, and finally said, all a-tremble, that the girl was *little Marie at La Guillette's place*.

Great was the surprise of Mère Maurice – this was the last girl she would have thought of. But she was considerate enough not to show her astonishment, and to keep her thoughts to herself. Then, seeing that her silence was weighing heavily on Germain, she held out her basket, saying:

'So is that any reason for not giving me a hand? Carry this load, and come and talk to me. Have you thought it through, Germain? Is your mind really made up?'

'Oh dear, Mother, that's not the way to talk; my mind would be made up if I had any chance of success, but since there's no chance of her listening to me, I've just made up my mind to get over it, if I can.'

'And what if you can't?'

'Everything comes to an end, Mère Maurice; when the horse is too heavily laden, it falls, and when the ox has nothing to eat, it dies.'

'Do you mean to say that you'll die, if you don't succeed? God forbid, Germain! I don't like to hear a man like you saying things like that, since when he says them he really thinks them. You have plenty of courage, and any weakness is dangerous in strong people. Come on, get your hopes up. I can't imagine that a girl who lives in poverty, and who you're doing a great honour by courting, can possibly turn you down.'

'But that's just how it is: she *is* turning me down.'

'And what reasons does she give you?'

'That you've always been kind to her, that her family owes yours a great deal, and that she doesn't want to offend you by luring me away from marrying someone rich.'

'If she says that, she's proving she has a good heart, and it's decent of her. But by saying that to you, Germain, she's not going to cure you, since she probably says that she loves you, and that she'd marry you if we were willing?'

'That's the worst of it! She says that she isn't attracted to me in her heart.'

'If she says what she doesn't really think, so as to keep you more effectively at arm's length, she's a child who deserves our love, and we can overlook her youth because she's being so very sensible.'

'Yes!' said Germain, struck by a new and hopeful idea that he had not dreamt of previously, 'that would be really sensible of her, just the *right* thing to do! But if she is so sensible, I'm afraid it's because she doesn't find me attractive.'

'Germain,' said Mère Maurice, 'I want you to promise me to keep your head down all week, stop tormenting yourself and start eating and sleeping and being cheerful like you used to be. I'll have a word with my old man, and if I can get him to agree, you'll know what the girl really feels about you.'

Germain promised, and the week went by without Père Maurice

saying anything out of the ordinary to him or seeming to suspect anything. The ploughman forced himself to appear calm, but he continued to grow even paler and more harassed.

Finally, on Sunday morning, after Mass, his mother-in-law asked him what he had got out of his young friend since the conversation in the orchard.

'But nothing at all,' he replied. 'I haven't spoken to her.'

'So how do you expect to win her over if you don't talk to her?'

'I've only spoken to her once,' replied Germain. 'It was when we were together at Fourche, and ever since that time, I haven't said a single word to her. Her refusal hurt me so much that I prefer not to hear her telling me all over again that she doesn't love me.'

'Well, son, you need to talk to her now; your father-in-law is giving his permission for you to do so. Go on, take the plunge! That's my advice and, if needs be, those are my orders; you can't go on like this, not knowing.'

Germain obeyed. He arrived at La Guillette's, his head bowed, looking crushed. Little Marie was sitting alone by the fireside, so wrapped up in thought that she did not hear Germain come in. When she saw him sitting in front of her, she jumped with surprise on her chair, and flushed crimson.

'Little Marie,' he said, sitting down next to her, 'I'm going to hurt and offend you, I know: but *the man and woman who live at ours*' (thereby designating the heads of the family) 'want me to talk to you and ask you to marry me. You don't want to, and I'm expecting a no.'

'So, Germain,' replied little Marie, 'it's quite true that you love me, then?'

'It annoys you, I know, but it's not my fault; if you could change your mind, I'd be happy, but I probably don't deserve it. Go on, Marie, look at me – am I really awful?'

'No, Germain,' she replied, with a smile, 'you're better-looking than me.'

'Don't tease; look at me with a bit of kindness; I haven't lost a single hair yet, or a tooth. My eyes will tell you I love you. So look into my eyes, it's written there, and any girl can read that writing.'

Marie gazed into Germain's eyes with her playful self-assurance, then, suddenly, she turned her head away and started to tremble.

'Oh God, I frighten you!' said Germain, 'you're looking at me as if I were the farmer from Les Ormeaux. Don't be afraid of me, please, it hurts too much. *I'm* not going to say nasty things to you; I won't kiss you if you don't want me to, and when you want me to go away, you need only show me the door. Look, do I have to leave to make you stop trembling?'

Marie held out her hand to the ploughman, but without turning her head away from the hearth, and without uttering a word.

'I understand,' said Germain; 'you're feeling sorry for me, as you're so kind; you're upset about making me unhappy, but can you really not love me?'

'Why are you saying these things to me, Germain?' little Marie finally replied. 'Do you really want to make me cry?'

'Poor little girl, you've got a good heart, I know; but you don't love me, and you're hiding your face away from me since you're frightened of letting me see your dislike and disgust. And I daren't even squeeze your hand! In the wood, when my son was asleep, and you were too, I almost gave you a little kiss. But I'd have died of shame rather than ask you, and I suffered as much that night as a man being roasted over a slow fire. Ever since, I've dreamt of you every night. Ah, how I kissed you then, Marie! But all that time, you were fast asleep and not dreaming. And now, do you know what I think? If only you'd turn round to look at me the way I look at you, and if only you could bring your face up to mine, I think I'd drop dead with joy. But you think that if anything similar happened to you, you'd die of anger and shame!'

Germain was speaking as if in a dream, without hearing what he was saying. Little Marie was still trembling, but as he was trembling even more, he no longer noticed her tremulousness. Suddenly she turned round; her eyes were streaming with tears, and gazing at him reproachfully. The poor ploughman thought that this was the last straw, and without waiting to hear his doom, he rose to depart; but the young girl stopped him, enfolding him in her arms, and hiding her head in his chest, she said, sobbing:

'Ah, Germain! Haven't you guessed that I love you?'

Germain would have gone quite crazy if his son who was out looking for him, and who came galloping into the cottage astride a pole, with his sister riding behind him, whipping with a wicker branch his imaginary courser, had not brought him back to his senses. He lifted him in his arms and, placing him in his fiancée's arms, said to her:

'Look! You've made more than one person happy by giving me your love!'

APPENDIX
THE COUNTRY WEDDING

So ends the story of Germain's marriage, as he told it me himself, skilful ploughman that he is! I must ask your pardon, Reader, for not having translated it better, for that is what the ancient and naive language spoken by the peasants of whom I sing (as they said in days of yore) needs: a real translation. Those folk speak French too well for us and, since Rabelais and Montaigne, the progress made by the language has made us lose many old treasures. So it is with all forms of progress; we need to resign ourselves to them. But it is still a pleasure to hear these picturesque idioms reigning over the old soil at the centre of France, especially as it is the authentic expression of the serenely mocking and amusingly garrulous character of the people who use it. Touraine has preserved a certain valuable number of patriarchal turns of phrase. But Touraine became thoroughly civilised during, and after, the Renaissance. It was covered with chateaux, roads, strangers and movement. The Berry area has stood still, and I believe that after Brittany and a few provinces of the extreme south of France, it is the *best-preserved* region around right now. Certain customs are so strange, so curious, that I hope to keep your interest for a few more minutes, dear Reader, if you will allow me to describe a country wedding to you, in detail – Germain's, for instance, at which I had the pleasure to be present a few years ago.

For, alas, everything passes away! Even within my own lifetime, there has been a bigger upheaval in the ideas and customs of my village than had been seen during all the centuries before the Revolution. Already, half the Celtic, pagan or medieval ceremonies that I saw still flourishing in my childhood have become obsolete. In another year or two, perhaps, the railways will be ploughing their way through our deep valleys, sweeping away, as quick as a flash, our ancient traditions and our wonderful legends.

It was in winter, around carnival-time, a season when it is quite the done thing to celebrate a wedding in our part of the world. In summer, people hardly have the time, and farm labours can barely tolerate three days' delay, not to mention the supplementary days allowed for the more or less laborious digestion of the psychological and physical intoxication that you suffer after a party. – I was sitting under the vast mantelpiece of an old kitchen chimney, when pistol-shots, howling dogs, and the shrill sounds of the bagpipes told me that the fiancés were approaching. Soon Père and Mère Maurice, Germain and little Marie, followed by Jacques and his wife, the main relatives on both sides and the godfathers and godmothers of the fiancés, made their entry into the yard.

Little Marie had not yet received the wedding presents, called the *livrées*[11], and she was dressed in the best clothes she could find from her modest and ragged wardrobe: a dress of dark, coarse cloth, a white shawl with a broad foliage pattern in showy colours, an apron of *incarnadine*, a red calico that was the height of fashion in those days and is now disdained, and a coif of very white muslin, in that shape that has happily been preserved, recalling as it does the coifs worn by Anne Boleyn and Agnès Sorel.[12] She was fresh and smiling, not in the least proud, although she had every reason to be so. Germain was serious and affectionate next to her, like the young Jacob greeting Rachel at the wells of Laban.[13] Any other girl would have assumed a self-important air and a triumphant demeanour, for at every level of society, it is quite something to be married for one's lovely eyes. But this young girl's eyes were moist and gleaming with tenderness; it was easy to see that she was deeply in love, and that she did not have the time to bother about what others thought. Her air of gentle firmness had not left her; but she was all openness and goodwill, and there was nothing impertinent in her success, nothing personal in her sense of strength. Never did I see such a nice, kind fiancée, as when she replied straightforwardly to her girlfriends who kept asking her if she was happy:

'Good heavens! Of course! I can't complain at the way the good Lord has treated me.'

Père Maurice was the general spokesman; he came up to utter the usual compliments and issue the usual invitations. He first tied to the mantelpiece a branch of laurel bedecked with ribbons – this is called the *exploit*[14], in other words the letter of invitation – then he handed round to all the guests a little cross made of a strip of blue ribbon with another strip of pink ribbon tied across it – the pink is for the fiancée, the blue for the man marrying her – and the guests, both men and women, had to keep this sign to decorate either their buttonhole or their wimple respectively on the day of the wedding. It acts as the letter of admission, the entrance ticket.

Then Père Maurice gave his speech. He invited the master of the household and all *his company*, in other words all his children, all his relatives, all his friends and all his servants, to the blessing, *to the feast, to the party-night, to the dancery, and to all that follows.* He did not forget to say, 'I have come to *do you the honour of summonsing you.*' This expression is perfectly apt, even though it seems wrong to us, since it conveys the idea of doing honour to those one thinks worthy of summoning in this way.

Despite the generosity of the invitation that is thus taken from house to house throughout the parish, politeness, which is extremely discreet among peasants, means that only two persons in each family profit from it – one head of the family from the household, and one of their children from the greater number.

Once these invitations had been issued, the fiancés and their relatives went to have dinner together at the farm.

Little Marie kept her three sheep on the commons, and Germain worked the land as if nothing unusual was afoot.

The eve of the day set apart for the wedding, around two o'clock in the afternoon, the music arrived, in other words the *bagpiper* and the *hurdy-gurdy man*, with their instruments decorated with long floating ribbons, and playing a march suitable for the occasion, to a rhythm that would seem rather slow to feet that were not from this part of the world, but perfectly in harmony with the nature of the fertile terrain and the rolling roads of the region.

Pistol-shots fired by the young men and the children announced the start of the wedding. People gradually assembled, and they danced on the lawn outside the house to get themselves into the swing of things. When night fell, they started to make strange preparations, separating into two bands, and after dark they proceeded to the ceremony of the *livrées*.

This happened in the house of the fiancée, La Guillette's cottage. La Guillette took her daughter with her, as well as a dozen young and pretty *shepherdlasses*, friends and relatives of her daughter, two or three respectable matrons, neighbours with the gift of the gab, quick with their replies, and the rigid guardians of ancient uses. Then she chose a dozen vigorous champions, her friends and relatives; finally the old *hemp crusher* of the parish, an eloquent man and a fine talker if ever there was one.

The role that in Brittany is played by the *bazvalan*[15], the village tailor, is in our country districts played by the hemp crusher or wool carder (two professions often performed by one man). You find him at every solemnity, whether sad or merry, since he is essentially a learned man and a fine talker, and on these occasions he is always given the task of acting as general spokesman so as worthily to perform certain formalities that have been customary from time immemorial. Professions where a man has to go from place to place and enter other people's households without being able to stay for any length of time in his own tend to make him chatty, witty, a good storyteller and singer.

The hemp crusher is particularly sceptical. He and another rustic official, whom I will be mentioning shortly, namely the gravedigger, are always the freethinkers in the region. They have spoken so much about ghosts and they are so conversant with all the tricks that such evil spirits can get up to that they have little fear of them. It is particularly at night time that all of them, gravediggers, hemp crushers and ghosts, get down to work. It is also at night that the hemp crusher relates his lugubrious legends. I hope I may here be permitted a digression.

When the hemp is finally *done*, in other words sufficiently wetted in the running waters and half dried on the *river-bank*, it is brought back into the yards of the houses; it is set upright in little sheaves which, with their stalks separated at the bottom and their heads bound together into balls, already somewhat resemble, when evening falls, a long procession of little white phantoms, perched on their spindly legs, and walking noiselessly along the walls.

It is at the end of September, when the nights are still warm, that by the pale moonlight they start to crush the hemp. During the daytime, the hemp has been heated in the oven; in the evening it is taken out so as to be ground while still hot. For this, they use a sort of trestle topped by a wooden lever which, falling back onto the grooves, crushes the plant without cutting it. It is then that you can hear, at night-time, out in the countryside, that dry, staccato sound of three blows being rapidly struck. Then there is a silence; this is when the hemp worker's arm pulls back the handful of hemp to crush it along another stretch of its length. And the three blows are heard again; it is the other arm pulling the lever, and so it continues, until the moon is veiled in the first glimmerings of dawn. Since this job occupies only a few days of the year, the dogs never get used to it and emit plaintive howls to every point of the horizon.

This is the time of unusual and mysterious noises in the countryside. Migrating cranes pass over regions where, in broad daylight, your eye can barely make them out. At night, you cannot see them, only hear them; and those raucous, lamenting voices, lost in the clouds, seem like the call and the farewell of tormented souls trying to find their way back to heaven, but forced by an invincible destiny to hover not far from the earth, around the dwellings of men; for these travelling birds suffer from strange uncertainties and mysterious anxieties in the course of their aerial crossing. Sometimes they lose the wind, when capricious breezes are locked in struggle or follow on after one another in the upper regions. Then, when these routs occur during the daytime, you see the leader of the flock floating in the air haphazardly, then wheeling round and coming back to place himself at the tail of the triangular phalanx, while a skilful manoeuvre on the part of his companions soon lines them all up in good order behind him. Often, after vain efforts, the exhausted guide abandons the attempt to lead the caravan; another comes forward, tries in his turn, and yields his place to a third, who manages to get back into the wind current and sets victoriously off on his march. But what cries, what reproaches, what rebukes, what savage curses and anxious questions are exchanged, in an unknown language, between these winged pilgrims!

In the echo-filled night, you sometimes hear these sinister clamours sweeping round for some considerable time over the houses, and since you cannot see anything, you feel in spite of yourself a sort of fear and shared unease, until that sobbing cloud has lost itself in the immensity.

There are yet other noises which you hear at this time of the year, usually in the orchards. The fruit has not yet been gathered, and a thousand unusual cracklings make the trees resemble living creatures. A branch creaks as it bows under a fruit that has suddenly reached its maximum weight, or else an apple breaks off and falls at your feet with a dull thud onto the damp earth. Then you can hear running off, as it brushes through the branches and the grass, a creature that you cannot see; it's the peasant's dog, that curious prowler, all on edge, both insolent and cowardly, gliding everywhere, never sleeping, always searching for who knows what, and spying on you, hidden in the undergrowth, only to take flight at the sound of the falling apple, thinking that you are throwing a stone at him.

It is during these nights – overcast and grey-clouded nights – that the hemp crusher relates his strange adventures with will-o'-the-wisps and white hares, souls in purgatory and sorcerers transformed into wolves, sabbaths at the crossroads and prophetic tawny owls in the cemetery. I remember having spent the first hours of the night in this way around active *crushers*, whose remorseless percussion, interrupting the hemp crusher's story at the most terrible place, made a cold shudder run through our veins. And often, too, the good man would continue to speak as he ground his hemp, and there were between four and five words that we did not pick up: fearful words, no doubt, that we did not dare ask him to repeat, and the omission of which added an even more dreadful mystery to the already dark mysteries of his tale. It was in vain that the maids warned us that it was very late to be still outdoors, and that the hour for sleep had long since chimed for us; they, too, were dying to carry on listening; and with what terror, thereafter, did we cross the hamlet to return home! How deep the porch of the church seemed to us, and how dense and black the shadow of the old trees! As for the cemetery, we did not see it; we closed our eyes as we skirted it.

But the hemp crusher is no more exclusively devoted to the pleasure of frightening people than is the sacristan; he likes to make people laugh, he can be mocking and sentimental as required, when he needs to sing of love and the nuptial bond; it is he who gathers and preserves the most ancient songs in his memory, and transmits them to posterity. So it is he whose responsibility it is, at wedding feasts, to play the role that we are about to see him perform at the presentation of the *livrées* to little Marie.

When everyone had gathered in the house, they closed, with the greatest care, the doors and windows; they even went to barricade the skylight of the granary; they placed planks, trestles, beams and tables across all entrances and exits, as if they were preparing to withstand a siege, and within this fortified interior there was an expectant and rather solemn silence until they heard, in the distance, songs, laughter, and the sound of rustic instruments. It was the band accompanying the bridegroom, with Germain himself at its head, leading his boldest companions, with the gravedigger, friends, relatives and servants, all forming a solid and merry procession.

However, as they approached the house, they slowed down, conferred together, and fell silent. The young girls locked inside the house had made small slits for themselves in the windows, through which they saw them coming up and deploying in battle order. A thin, cold rain was falling, which added to the piquancy of the situation, while a big fire was crackling in the grate. Marie would have liked to shorten the inevitable slowness and tedium of this customary siege; she did not like to see her fiancé having to cool his heels like this, but on this occasion she had no say in the matter, and indeed was obliged to share quite openly in the rebellious cruelty of her girlfriends.

When the two camps were thus arrayed opposite each other, a discharge of firearms from outside set off all the dogs in the environs. The house dogs rushed to the door, barking loudly, thinking that a real attack was underway, and the small children, whom their mothers attempted in vain to reassure, started to cry and tremble. This whole scene was so well played that a stranger would have been quite taken in, and might perhaps have thought it a good idea to prepare his defences against a band of incendiaries.

Then the gravedigger, the bard and orator of the fiancé, took up his position in front of the door, and, in a voice of lamentation, struck up with the hemp crusher, placed at the skylight that was situated above this same door, the following dialogue:

GRAVEDIGGER: Alas! My good people, my dear parishioners, for the love of God, open the door to me.

HEMP CRUSHER: And who may you be, and why are you making so bold as to call us your dear parishioners? We do not know you.

GRAVEDIGGER: We are decent folk and we are suffering. Do not be afraid of us, my friends! Give us your hospitality. Black ice is falling, our poor feet are frozen, and we have come from so far away that our clogs have split.

HEMP CRUSHER: If your clogs are split, you can look around on the ground; you will soon see a twig or two of osier wicker to make *lacelets* (little strips of iron in the shape of bows that are tied round split clogs to make them stronger).

GRAVEDIGGER: Lacelets of wicker are not very strong. You mock us, good people, and you would do better to open the door to us. We can see a fine flame gleaming in your home; no doubt you have set the spit turning, and at yours there is good cheer for both heart and belly. So open up for poor pilgrims who will die at your door if you do not show them mercy.

HEMP CRUSHER: Aha! So you are pilgrims? You had not told us that. And from what pilgrimage have you come, if you please?

GRAVEDIGGER: We will tell you that when you have opened the door to us, since we come from so far away that you would be unwilling to believe us.

HEMP CRUSHER: Open the door to you? Oh yes! We do not trust you. Let us see: is it from Saint-Sylvain de Pouligny that you come?

GRAVEDIGGER: We *have* been to Saint-Sylvain de Pouligny, but we have been even further than that.

HEMP CRUSHER: So you have been as far as Sainte-Solange?

GRAVEDIGGER: Sainte-Solange, yes, we have been there, indeed, but we have been even further than that.

HEMP CRUSHER: You are lying; you have never even been as far as Sainte-Solange.

GRAVEDIGGER: We *have* been further, for, right now, we are returning from Santiago da Compostela.

HEMP CRUSHER: What is that nonsense you are telling us? We do not know that parish. We can see that you are wicked people, brigands, *good-for-nothings* and liars. Go and sing your silly songs elsewhere; we are on our guard, and you will not enter here within.

GRAVEDIGGER: Alas! My poor man, have pity on us! We are not pilgrims, you guessed right; we are wretched poachers pursued by the gamekeepers. Even the gendarmes are after us and, if you do not hide us in your hayloft, we will be caught and taken off to jail.

HEMP CRUSHER: And who will prove this time that you are indeed what you say you are? There is already one lie you have not been able to get away with.

GRAVEDIGGER: If you will open to us, we will show you a fine piece of game that we have killed.

HEMP CRUSHER: Show it straight away, for we are filled with mistrust.

GRAVEDIGGER: Very well, open a door or a window, so we can pass the beast into you.

HEMP CRUSHER: No, you don't! We are not so stupid! I can spy you through a little hole! And I see among you neither hunters, nor game.

At this point an apprentice oxherd, thickset and endowed with Herculean strength, stepped out of the group where he had been standing unnoticed, and raised towards the skylight a plucked goose skewered on a strong iron skewer, decorated with straw bouquets and ribbons.

'Oh yes!' exclaimed the hemp crusher, after passing his arm out to give the roast a cautious feel; 'this is neither a quail, nor a partridge; it is something like a goose or a turkey. Truly, you are fine hunters! And this game here did not make you run very fast! Go elsewhere, you foolish folk! All your lies are known, and you can go off to your own homes to get your supper cooked for you. You are not going to eat ours.'

GRAVEDIGGER: Alas! My God, where will we go to cook our game? There is not much here, given that there are so many of us, and in any case, we have neither fire nor shelter. At this hour all doors are shut, everyone is in bed; only you are making merry in your house, and you must be very hard-hearted to leave us here freezing to death outside. Open up, good folk, once more; we will not cause you any expense. You can see we have brought you the roast; just a little place by your

97

fireside, a little flame to cook it, and we will leave fully content.

HEMP CRUSHER: Do you think we have room to spare in our home, and that the wood costs us nothing?

GRAVEDIGGER: Here we have a little bale of straw to make a fire – we will make do with that; just give us permission to lay the spit across your fireplace.

HEMP CRUSHER: That will not be; you fill us with disgust and not at all with pity. I see that you are drunk, that you need nothing, and that you want to get into our house to steal our fire and our daughters.

GRAVEDIGGER: Since you will not hear any good reason, we will enter your house by force.

HEMP CRUSHER: Try, if you want to. We are well enough protected not to fear you. And since you are insolent folk, we will not reply to you further.

Whereupon the hemp crusher slammed down the shutter of the skylight, and climbed down a ladder into the room beneath. Then he again took the fiancée by her hand, and the young people of both sexes joined them, and proceeded to dance and shout merrily, while the matrons sang in piercing tones, and roared with laughter out of bravado and contempt for those outside who were attempting the assault.

The besiegers, on their side, had unleashed their fury: they were discharging their pistols into the doors, making the dogs growl, banging fiercely against the walls, rattling the shutters and uttering fearsome cries – in short, raising such a din you could not hear yourself speak, and kicking up such a cloud of dust and smoke you could not see a thing.

And yet this attack was all feigned; the time had not yet come to violate the ceremonial. If it was possible by prowling around to find an unguarded passage, some opening or other, you could try to sneak in and then, if the bearer of the roast managed to place his roast on the fire, the capture of the hearth was acknowledged, the little drama was over, and the fiancé was the winner.

But the ways into the house were not so numerous that people had neglected the usual precautions, and nobody would have assumed the right to use violence before the time fixed for the fight.

When they got tired of jumping and shouting, the hemp crusher decided to capitulate. He climbed back up to his skylight, opened it cautiously, and greeted the disappointed besiegers with a burst of laughter.

'Well, lads!' he said, 'you look pretty sheepish! You thought there was nothing easier than to get in here, and as you can see, our defences are good. But we're starting to feel sorry for you, if you are ready to yield and accept our conditions.'

GRAVEDIGGER: Speak, good people; say what it is we need to do to approach your hearth.

HEMP CRUSHER: You must sing, my friends, but you must sing a song that we do not know, and to which we cannot respond by singing a better one.

'That's no obstacle!' replied the gravedigger.

And he struck up, in a powerful voice:

'*Six months ago the spring was here…*'

'*I strode among the growing grass,*' replied the hemp crusher, in a somewhat hoarse but still awe-inspiring voice. 'Are you making fun of us, my poor people, singing such an old-fashioned piece? As you see, we can stop you at the very first word!'

'*She was a prince's daughter fair…*'

'*Who sought a husband for herself,*' replied the hemp crusher. 'Go on, try another one! We know that one all too well.'

GRAVEDIGGER: Do you want this one? *As I came back from Nantes one day…*

HEMP CRUSHER: *I was a weary, weary man!* That one dates from my grandmother's time. Try another one!

GRAVEDIGGER: *The other day as I took the air…*

HEMP CRUSHER: *Along this wood all sweet and fair!* Now that one's really silly! Our little children couldn't be bothered to reply to that one! So is that all you know?

GRAVEDIGGER: Oh, we'll sing so many to you that you won't be able to keep up.

A good hour went by in this jousting. As the two protagonists knew more songs than anyone in the land, with a seemingly inexhaustible repertoire, it might have lasted all night long, especially since the hemp crusher maliciously enjoyed allowing his rival to sing certain complaints in ten, twenty or thirty couplets, pretending, by his silence, to declare himself beaten. Then they started triumphing in the fiancé's camp; they chorused the words at the tops of their voices, and this time they thought that the other side would fail to respond, but halfway through the final couplet, they heard the rough, pinched voice of the old hemp crusher bellowing out the last words, after which he cried:

'No need to tire yourselves out singing such a long one, my little friends! We already had it at our fingertips!'

Once or twice, however, the hemp crusher pulled a face, frowned, and turned round with a disappointed air to the attentive matrons. The gravedigger was singing something so old that his adversary had forgotten it, or perhaps had never known it, but immediately the good women struck up, in their nasal voices, mewing like seagulls, the victorious refrain, and the gravedigger, commanded to surrender, moved on to the next try.

It would have taken too long to wait and see which side would win. The fiancée's side declared that they would let the other side off so long as they offered her a present worthy of her.

Then began the song of the *livrées*, to a tune as solemn as a hymn.

The men outside sang in their big bass voices, in unison:

> *Open the door now, open up*
> *Marie, my darling girl,*
> *I done got fine presents for you with me here*
> *Alas! So let us in right now, my dear.*

To which the women replied from within, in falsetto, and in a tone of lament:

> *My father is sorrowful, my mother filled with sadness,*
> *And I am a girl too full of mercy*
> *To open my door at this hour of the day.*

The men repeated the first couplet up to the fourth verse, which they modified as follows:

> *I done got a nice hanky for you here.*

But, in the name of the fiancée, the women replied the same way they had the first time round.

Over twenty couplets, at least, the men enumerated all the presents of the *livrée*, always mentioning a new object in the last verse: a *fine front* (apron), lovely ribbons, an outfit of cloth, some lace, a gold cross and even *a hundred pins* to complete the bride's modest basket of gifts. The matrons' refusal was irrevocable, but eventually the boys decided to speak of *a fine husband for you here*, and the women replied, turning to the bride, and singing to her, with the men:

> *Open the door now, open up,*
> *Marie, my darling girl,*
> *It's a fine husband coming to seek you here,*
> *So come on, let them in right now, my dear.*

3
The Wedding

Thereupon, the hemp crusher pulled the wooden peg that closed the door from the interior; this was still, at that time, the only lock known in most of the dwellings in our hamlet. The fiancé's band erupted into the fiancée's home, but not without a fight, for the boys stationed in the house, even the old hemp crusher and the old gossips, felt duty-bound to guard the hearth. The carrier of the spit, supported by his own side, had to succeed in planting the roast in the hearth. It was a real battle, although people abstained from actually hitting one another, and there was no anger in their struggle. But they pushed and squeezed so hard, and there was so much self-esteem at stake in this matching of muscular strength with strength, that the results could be more serious than they appeared from the laughter and songs. The poor old hemp crusher, who was fighting like a lion, was glued to the wall and hemmed in by the crowd, so much that he could hardly breathe. More than one toppled champion was accidentally crushed underfoot, more than one hand clutching at the spit was bloodied. These games are dangerous, and accidents in recent times have become so serious that our peasants have resolved to let the ceremony of the *livrées* fall into abeyance. I think that we saw the last of them at the wedding of Françoise Meillant, and even there the struggle was only feigned.

It was still quite a passionate affair at Germain's wedding. On both sides it was a matter of honour, either to invade or to defend La Guillette's hearth and home. The enormous iron spit was twisted like a vice in the sturdy hands that were wrestling for its possession. A pistol-shot set fire to a small store of hemp dolls, set on a wicker rack, on the ceiling. This incident caused a diversion, and while some were busy putting out what might have turned into a real fire, the gravedigger, who had climbed up into the granary without anyone noticing, came down the chimney and seized the spit just as the oxherd, who was standing defending it at the hearth, was holding it over his head to prevent it being wrested away from him. Some time before the capture, the matrons had taken care to extinguish the fire, in case, while people were fighting next to it, someone managed to fall onto it and get burnt. The facetious gravedigger, in cahoots with the oxherd, thus managed to seize the trophy without difficulty and set it across the *firedogs*. It was all over! No one was allowed to touch it any more. He bounded into the middle of the room and lit a remnant of straw that was lying round the spit so as to mimic the roasting of the goose, as the latter lay all in pieces bestrewing the floor with its dispersed limbs.

Then there was an outburst of laughter and swaggering arguments. Everyone showed off the bumps and bruises he had received, and since it was often the hand of a friend that had struck him, nobody complained or quarrelled. The hemp crusher, half flattened, was rubbing the small of his back, saying that he didn't really care a hoot, but that he had to protest against the trick played by his colleague the gravedigger – and that, if he hadn't been half dead, the hearth would not have been conquered so easily. The matrons swept the floor, and order was gradually restored. The table was set with ewers of new wine. When they had clinked glasses together and drawn their breath, the fiancé was brought into the middle of the room and, armed with a rod, he was forced to submit to a new ordeal.

During the struggle, the fiancée had been concealed with three of her girlfriends by her mother, her godmother and her aunts, who had made the four young girls sit on a bench, in a far corner of the room, and had covered them with a big white cloth. The three friends had all been chosen because they were the same build as Marie, and their wimples of the same height, so that as the cloth covered them from head to foot, it was impossible to distinguish between them.

The fiancé was allowed to touch them only with the tip of his rod, and only in order to designate the one he judged to be his wife. He was given time to examine them, but only with his eyes, and the matrons, standing at his side, kept close watch to make sure he did not cheat. If he made a mistake, he would not be able to dance that evening with his fiancée, but only with the girl he had chosen by mistake.

Germain, finding himself in the presence of these phantoms enveloped under the same shroud, was very much afraid of getting it wrong; and indeed, this had happened to many other men, since precautions were always laid with conscientious care. His heart was beating. Little Marie did indeed try to breathe heavily and move the cloth a little, but her malicious rivals did exactly the same, poking the cloth with their fingers, and there were as many mysterious signals being sent as there were young girls under the veil. Their square wimples held up this veil so uniformly that it was impossible to see the shape of a forehead outlined by its folds.

Germain, after ten minutes of hesitation, closed his eyes, commended his soul to God, and held out his rod at random. He touched the forehead of little Marie, who threw off the cloth, crying victory. Then he was given permission to kiss her and, sweeping her up in his strong arms, he carried her into the middle of the room, and opened the dance with her. It lasted until two in the morning.

Then they went their separate ways as they were to reassemble at eight o'clock. Since there were several young people who had come in from the surrounding district, and not enough beds for everyone, every female guest from the village took into her bed two or three girlfriends, while the boys went off pell-mell to stretch out on the forage in the farm granary. As you can well imagine, they hardly slept while they were there, since the only idea in their heads was to play pranks on one another, to exchange jeers and tell each other crazy stories. At weddings, it is obligatory to go without sleep for three nights – nobody minds.

At the time agreed for the departure, after we had all eaten soup with milk, flavoured with a strong dose of pepper to get our appetites up, since the wedding meal promised to be copious, we gathered again in the farmyard. Since our parish had been suppressed, we had to go half a league away for the nuptial blessing. It was a fine, fresh day, but the roads were still very bad, so everyone had come along with a horse, and each man took up behind his saddle a woman, old or young. Germain set off on Grey who, well groomed, newly shod and decked out with ribbons, was champing at the bit and breathing fire through her nostrils. He went to fetch his fiancée from the cottage with his brother-in-law Jacques who, mounted on Old Grey, took good Mother La Guillette behind the saddle, while Germain went back into the farmyard, bringing his dear little wife, with an air of triumph.

Then the merry cavalcade set off, escorted on foot by the children, who were running along letting off pistol-shots and making the horses jump. Mère Maurice was sitting in a little wagon with Germain's three children and the village fiddlers. They headed the march to the sound of their instruments. Petit-Pierre looked so handsome that his old grandmother was filled with pride. But the impetuous child did not stay at her side for long. When once they came to a halt, halfway to their destination, before embarking on a difficult stretch of road, he slipped away and went over to beg his father to sit him in front of him, on Grey.

'Oh, yes!' replied Germain. 'People will soon start making horrid jokes! We mustn't.'

'I really don't care what the people from Saint-Chartier will say,' said little Marie. 'Take him, Germain, please; I'll be even more proud of him than I am of my wedding dress.'

Germain gave in, and the handsome trio galloped into place, triumphantly borne by Grey.

And indeed, the people from Saint-Chartier, although very mocking and inclined to tease those from the surrounding parishes amalgamated with theirs, did not dream of laughing when they saw such a handsome groom, such a pretty bride and a child who would have filled a king's daughter with longing. Petit-Pierre was wearing a full suit of cornflower blue, and a red waistcoat so dainty and short that it hardly came down any lower than his chin. The village tailor had sewn the armholes so tight that he could hardly bring his two arms together. And how proud he was! He had a round hat with black and gold braid, and a peacock feather emerging with a swagger from a tuft of guinea-fowl feathers. A bouquet of flowers, bigger than his head, covered his shoulders, and ribbons were floating down to his feet. The hemp crusher, who was also the local barber and wig-maker, had cut his hair level, covering his head with a basin and chopping off everything that stuck out – an infallible method for a neat haircut. Thus attired, the poor child was less poetic, to be sure, than with his long hair in the wind and his sheepskin coat *à la* John the Baptist, but he did not think so in the least, and everyone admired him, saying he looked like a real little man. His beauty triumphed over everything and, indeed, what would the incomparable beauty of childhood *not* triumph over?

His little sister Solange was wearing, for the first time in her life, a wimple in place of the calico bonnet that little girls wear until the age of two or three years. And what a wimple! Higher and wider than the poor thing's entire body. And how beautiful she thought she looked! She did not dare to turn her head, and held herself stiff and upright, thinking that everyone would imagine she was the bride.

As for little Sylvain, he was still in his fine costume – and, asleep on his grandmother's knees, he had little idea of what a wedding was.

Germain gazed fondly at his children and, on his arrival at the *mairie*, he said to his fiancée:

'Look, Marie, I'm a bit happier coming here today than I was when I brought you back to ours, from the Chanteloube woods, thinking that you'd never love me; I took you in my arms to lower you down to the ground just like now; but I though that we'd never see each other again, on poor, good old Grey, with this child on our knees. You know, I love you so much, and I love these children so much, I'm so happy that you love me and that you love them, and that my parents love you, and I love your mother and my friends so much, I love everybody so much today, that I'd like to have three or four hearts to contain all my love. It's true that one isn't room enough for so much friendship and so much happiness! It gives me a kind of stomach-ache.'

There was a crowd gathered at the doors of the *mairie* and the church to gaze at the pretty bride. Why shouldn't we describe her costume? It suited her so well! Her wimple of clear muslin, embroidered all over, had its pinners bedecked with lace. In those days, peasant women did not allow themselves to show a single hair, and even though they conceal under their wimples a magnificent head of hair all curled up in ribbons of white cotton to hold up the coif, even today it would be indecent and shameful for them to show themselves to men bareheaded. However, these days they do allow themselves to leave on their foreheads a narrow headband which greatly adds to their attractiveness. But I miss the classical hairstyle of my own day: that white lace standing out starkly against the skin had a kind of ancient chastity in their appearance that struck me as more solemn, and when a face was beautiful in this way, it was with a beauty whose charm and naive majesty were inexpressible.

Little Marie still wore her hair like that, and her forehead was so white and so pure that it defied the whiteness of the linen to darken it.

Although she hadn't had a wink of sleep all night, the morning air and especially the inner joy of a soul as limpid as the sky, and, in addition, a certain secret flame contained by the modesty of adolescence, brought to her cheeks a gleam as soft and gentle as the blossom of the peach tree in the first sunbeams of April.

Her white shawl, chastely tied over her breast, showed no more than the delicate outline of a neck as round as a turtle dove's; her negligee of fine cloth in myrtle green brought out what a petite figure she had – it seemed perfect, but it would inevitably grow and fill out, since she was not yet seventeen. She was wearing a silk apron as purple as a pansy, with the bib in place; our village women have made the mistake of getting rid of it, though it gave so much elegance and modesty to her bosom. Today, the women show off their shawl with more pride, but in their costume there is no longer that fine flower of ancient modesty that made them resemble the virgins of Holbein. They are more coquettish, more graceful. Good style, in bygone days, was a kind of severe stiffness which made their rare smiles seem deeper and more ideal.

At the offering, Germain, following the usual custom, placed the *treizain*, in other words thirteen coins, into his fiancée's hand. He slipped onto her finger a silver ring of a shape that had not changed for centuries, but which the *golden wedding ring* has now replaced. As they came out of the church, Marie murmured to him:

'So is this the ring that I wanted – the one that I asked you for, Germain?'

'Yes,' he replied, 'the one that my Catherine had on her finger when she died. It's the same ring for my two weddings.'

'Thank you, Germain,' said the young woman, in a serious tone of voice that expressed her emotion. 'I'll die with it, and if I die before you, you can keep it for the wedding of your little Solange.'

4
The Cabbage

We got back onto our horses and returned quickly to Belair. The meal was splendid and, interspersed with songs and dances, lasted until midnight. The old folks did not leave the table for a full fourteen hours. The gravedigger cooked the meal – very successfully. He had a reputation for his cooking, and he would leave the stove to come and join in with the dancing and singing in between each course. And yet he was an epileptic, poor old Bontemps! Who would have guessed it? He was as full of vigour, strength and good cheer as a young man. One day we discovered him as if dead, wracked by his illness and lying in a ditch, as night fell. We brought him home in a wheelbarrow, and spent the night looking after him. Three days later he was celebrating another wedding, singing like a thrush and gambolling like a lamb, hopping around in the time-honoured manner. On leaving a wedding, he would go to dig a grave and nail down a coffin. He fulfilled his task piously, and although his cheerful temper never betrayed the fact, it left him with a sinister impression which hastened the return of his fit. His wife, a paralytic, had not stirred from her chair for twenty years. Her mother is a hundred and four and still alive. But he, poor man, so merry, so kind, so amusing, got killed last year falling from his granary onto the cobbles. He was probably suffering from an attack, and, as usual, he had hidden himself away in the hay so as not to frighten and upset his family. In this way, he brought to a tragic end a life as strange as he himself was, a mixture of gloom and madcap antics, of terrible and laughable events, amidst which his heart had always remained kind and his character lovable.

But this brings us to the third day of the wedding festivities, which is the most curious of all, and has preserved its full rigour right up until today. I will pass over the piece of toast that they bring to the wedding bed: it's rather a silly custom which makes the bride's modesty suffer and tends to destroy that of the young girls who take part in it. In any case, I think it's a custom found in all our provinces, and one which is not particular to our part of the world.

Just as the ceremony of the *livrées* is the symbol of the capture of the heart and dwelling of the bride, that of the cabbage is the symbol of the marriage's fecundity. After lunch on the day after the wedding, this strange performance begins: it is of Gallic origin, but in being transmitted via primitive Christianity it has little by little become a sort of mystery, or farcical morality play from the Middle Ages.

Two boys (the most light-hearted and best-disposed in the band) disappear during the lunch, and go to get dressed up; finally they return, escorted by music, dogs, children and pistol-shots. They represent a couple of beggars, dressed in the most wretched rags and tatters. The husband is the dirtiest of the two: it is vice that has led to his degradation; his wife is merely wretched and brutalised by her husband's lack of self-control.

They call themselves *the gardener* and *the gardener's wife*, and say that they have been set to watch over and cultivate the sacred cabbage. But the husband bears different names which all have their meaning. He is called the *pailloux*, or *strawman*, since he wears on his head a wig of straw or hemp and, to conceal his nakedness barely covered by his rags, he wraps his legs and part of his body round with straw. He also makes for himself a big belly or a hump with straw or hay hidden under his smock. He is also called the *peilloux*, since he is covered with *peille* (or rags). And finally, the *païen*, or *pagan*, which is even more meaningful, since in his cynical opinions and his debauched way of life he is meant to represent a compendium of the antipodes of every Christian virtue.

He arrives, his face smeared with soot and the lees of wine, sometimes decked out with a grotesque mask. He uses a poor quality, cracked earthenware cup, or an old clog, hanging from his belt by a piece of string, to ask for alms of wine. Nobody refuses him, and he pretends to drink; then he spills the wine on the ground, as a libation. At every step, he keeps falling down and rolling in the mud; he pretends to be in prey to the most shameful drunkenness. His poor wife runs after him, picks him up, calls for help, tears out the shreds of hempen hair that stick out from her filthy wimple, weeps over her husband's abjection, and pours heart-rending reproaches on him.

'You wretch!' she tells him, 'just look where your bad behaviour has brought us! However much I sew and labour for you, and mend your clothes, you keep tearing them and getting yourself all mucky. You've squandered what little I had, our six children haven't a bean, we live in a cowshed with the animals; and now we're reduced to begging for alms, and you're so ugly, so repulsive, so despised that soon people will start throwing bread to us the way they do to dogs. Ah, my poor *worldlings* (my poor people), take pity on us! Take pity on me! I have not deserved my fate, and never did a wife have a filthier and more hateful husband. Help me to pick him up, otherwise the carts will crush him like a piece of old glass from a smashed bottle, and I'll be left a widow, which would just about finish me off – I'd die of grief, even though everyone says it would be the best thing that could happen to me.'

Such is the role of the gardener's wife and her continual lamentations throughout the performance. For that is what it is: a real play, unscripted, improvised, played in the open, on the roads, in the fields, drawing on all the fortuitous accidents that happen. Everyone participates in it: the wedding guests and those from outside, people staying in the village and those passing by along the roads, for three or four hours of the day, as we shall see. The theme is invariable, but on this basic theme an infinite number of variations are embroidered, and it is here that we are forced to recognise the instinct for mimicry, the abundance of farcical ideas, the gift of the gab, the spirit of repartee and even the natural eloquence of our peasants.

The role of the gardener's wife is usually given to a slim, beardless and fresh-complexioned man, one who is able to give his character a great deal of authenticity and can convey comic despair naturally enough for the spectators to be cheered and saddened by it at one and the same time, just as if it were something real. These skinny, beardless men are not rare in our countryside and, strange to relate, are often the more remarkable for the strength of their muscles.

Once the misfortune of the wife has been acknowledged, the young men at the wedding urge her to leave her drunken husband where he is, and to have a good time with them. They offer her their arms and drag her off. Little by little she yields, grows merry and starts to run around now with one chap, now with another, starting to act like a real hussy – a new morality play: the husband's misbehaviour leads to and explains that of his wife.

The *pagan* then wakes out of his drunken stupor, gazes round looking for his partner, arms himself with a rope and a stick, and runs after her. They make him run everywhere, they hide, they pass his wife from one man to the next, they try to keep her busy and to deceive her jealous husband. Her *men friends* endeavour to get her drunk. Finally he catches up with his unfaithful wife and tries to beat her. The most real and best-observed aspect in this parody of the miseries of married life is that the jealous man never attacks those who have made off with his wife. He is quite polite and prudent with them; he wants to take it out on the guilty party alone – since she is deemed to be unable to resist him.

But just as he is raising his stick and getting his rope ready to tie up the delinquent, all the men at the wedding intervene and throw themselves between the two spouses. *'Don't beat her! Never beat your wife!'* is the formula that is repeated ad nauseam in these scenes. They disarm the husband, who is forced to forgive and embrace his wife, and soon he affects to love her more than ever. Off he goes, arm in arm with her, singing and dancing until he is again overcome by drunkenness and starts rolling around on the ground, and then his wife's lamentations start up again, together with her discouragement, her feigned errings and strayings, her husband's jealousy, the neighbours' intervention and the patching up of relations between the two of them. In all this there is a naive, even coarse lesson, with a strong whiff of its origins in the Middle Ages, but one which always makes an impression, if not on married couples – too much in love or too sensible these days to need it – at least on children and teenagers. The pagan so frightens and repels the young girls when he runs after them and pretends to kiss them that they run away with an emotion that has nothing feigned about it. His smeared face and his big stick (however inoffensive it may be) make the kids squeal with fright. It's a comedy of manners in its most elementary, but also its most striking shape.

Once this farce is fully under way, they get ready to go and find the cabbage. They bring a stretcher on which they place the *pagan*, armed with a spade, a rope and a big basket. Four sturdy men carry him off on their shoulders. His wife follows him on foot, the *ancients* follow in a group after him, looking solemn and thoughtful; then the wedding party marches along in couples, stepping out to the rhythm of the music. The pistol-shots start up again, and the dogs howl more than ever at the sight of the filthy *pagan*, thus borne aloft in triumph. The children mockingly wave clogs dangling from lengths over him, as if wafting incense.

But why do they grant this ovation to such a repellent figure? They march to the conquest of the sacred cabbage, the emblem of matrimonial fecundity, and it is this drunken sot who alone can set his hand on the symbolic plant. Doubtless what we have here is some mystery that dates back to before Christianity and which recalls the feast of the Saturnalia, or some ancient bacchanal. Perhaps this *pagan*, who at the same time is the gardener par excellence, is no less than Priapus in person, the god of gardens and of debauchery, a divinity who must however have been chaste and serious in his origins, like the mystery of reproduction, even though licentious manners and decadent notions have imperceptibly degraded it.

Be that as it may, the triumphal march arrives at the dwelling of the bride, and makes its way into her garden. Here they choose the finest cabbage, which takes quite a while, since the elders take council and discuss the matter endlessly, each of them extolling the cabbage that strikes him as the most suitable. They put it to the vote, and when the choice has been fixed, the *gardener* ties his rope around the stem, and moves as far away as the length of the garden will permit him. The gardener's wife takes care that, in its fall, the sacred vegetable will not be damaged. The *Jokers* of the wedding, the hemp crusher, the gravedigger, the carpenter or the clog maker (all those, in fact, who do not till the soil and who, spending their lives in the houses of other people, are reputed to have – and really do have – more wit and a readier tongue than mere agricultural workers), gather in rows round the cabbage. One of them digs a trench with the spade, and makes it so deep that anyone would think they were going to chop down an oak tree. The other places on his nose a wooden or cardboard *drogue*, a peg designed to look like a pair of glasses; he is acting as the *engineer* – he comes up, walks away, draws up a plan, keeps a close eye on the workers, draws lines, gets pernickety, exclaims that they're going to spoil everything, makes them drop their work and then resume it at his whim, and, at the greatest length and in the most ridiculous way possible directs the enterprise. Is all this an addition to the ancient formula of the ceremony, a mockery of theorists in general – despised as they are by your ordinary peasant – or an expression of the hatred felt for the land surveyors who regulate the land registry and set the rate of tax, or, finally, of hatred for the officials of the highways department who convert common land into roads, and suppress age-old abuses dear to the peasants? The fact of the matter is that this character in the performance is indeed called the *géomètre*, or land surveyor, and he does his level best to make himself a thorough nuisance to all those who wield the mattock and the spade.

Finally, after a quarter of an hour filled with difficulties and mummery, so as not to cut the root of the cabbage and to dig it up without damaging it, whilst spadefuls of earth are chucked at the faces of those present (too bad for anyone who doesn't manage to get out of the way quickly enough; even if he were a bishop of a prince, he would still need to receive the baptism of the earth), the pagan pulls the rope, his wife holds out her apron, and the cabbage majestically falls to the acclamations of the spectators. Then they bring the basket, and the *pagan* couple plant the cabbage in it, with every care and precaution. It is surrounded with fresh earth, supported with rods and twine in the same way that flower sellers in towns arrange their splendid potted camellias; red apples are stuck onto the end of rods, with branches of thyme, sage and laurel all around; the whole is adorned with ribbons and banners; the trophy is loaded back onto the stretcher with the *pagan*, who has to keep it balanced and preserve it from any accidents, and eventually they march out of the garden in good order.

But as they come up to the door, just as when later they have to enter the yard of the bridegroom's house, an imaginary obstacle opposes their passage. The men carrying the burden stumble, utter loud exclamations, retreat, advance again and, as if repelled by some invincible force, pretend to succumb under its weight. Meanwhile, the onlookers shout out, urging on and restraining the humans bearing their load. 'Nicely does it, my lad! Come on now! Look out! Hang on a minute! Down a bit. The door's too low! Squeeze in together, it's too narrow! Left a bit; now right a bit! Come on, get stuck in now! You've done it!'

This is the way that in the years of abundant harvest, the ox cart, excessively laden with forage or corn, turns out to be too wide or too high to enter in through the big barn door. This is the way they shout after the robust animals to restrain them or urge them on; this is the way that, with a bit of skill and some vigorous efforts, they manage to get the mountain of riches under the rustic triumphal arch without tipping it all over. It is the last cartage in particular – called the *gerbaude*, or 'sheafage' – that requires these precautions, since this is also a rural festivity, and the last sheaf picked up from the last furrow is placed at the summit of the wagon, adorned with ribbons and flowers, just like the forehead of the oxen and the goad of the oxherd. Thus the triumphant and laborious entry of the cabbage into the house is a simulacrum of the prosperity and fecundity that it represents.

Once it has reached the yard of the bridegroom's house, the cabbage is taken away and carried up to the top of the house or the barn. If there is a chimney, a gable or a pigeon-loft higher than the other rooftops, the burden must be carried, whatever the risk, up to the topmost pinnacle of the building. The *pagan* accompanies it there, fixes it in place, and sprinkles a great ewer of wine all over it, while a volley of pistol-shots and joyful contortions on the part of his wife signal its inauguration.

The same ceremony then immediately starts up all over again. They go off to unearth another cabbage in the bridegroom's garden and bear it with the same formalities up onto the roof of the house his wife has just abandoned to follow him. These trophies remain there until the wind and the rain destroy the baskets and carry off the cabbage. But they dwell there long enough to give some chance of success to the prediction that the ancients and the matrons utter as they hail it. 'Fine cabbage,' they say, 'live and flourish, so that our young bride may have a lovely little child before the year is out; for if you happened to die too quickly it would be a sign of sterility, and you would be up there on her house like an ill omen.'

The day is already far gone before all these things are accomplished. All that is left is to see off the godfathers and godmothers of the newlyweds. When these putative relations live some way away, they are accompanied with music and the entire wedding party to the limits of the parish. There is some more dancing on the road, and they are kissed farewell. The *pagan* and his wife then have their faces washed and are given clean clothes, if they have not been so tired out by the roles they have been playing that they have had to go and take a nap.

They were still dancing, singing and eating at the Belair farm, at midnight on the third day of Germain's wedding party. The ancients, sitting at table, could not get away, and with good reason. They found their feet, and their wits, only when the next day dawned. Then, while they headed for their homes, staggering silently along, Germain, bright-eyed and bushy-tailed, proudly went out to yoke his oxen, leaving his young partner to doze on until sunrise. The lark, singing as it rose into the sky, seemed to him to be the voice of his own heart giving thanks to Providence. The hoar frost, glinting on the bare bushes, looked like the whiteness of April flowers just before the leaves come out. Everything in nature seemed to him to be filled with good cheer and serenity. Little Pierre had laughed and jumped so much the day before that he did not come along to help him drive his oxen; but Germain was happy to be alone. He knelt down in the furrow he was about to break anew, and made his morning prayer with such an outpouring of emotion that two tears trickled onto his cheeks still moist with sweat.

In the distance could be heard the songs of the boys from the neighbouring parishes as they set off home, repeating, in their somewhat hoarse voices, the joyful refrains of the previous day.

NOTES

1. This is a famous woodcut by Hans Holbein the Younger (1497–1543); the work is usually known in English as *The Dance of Death* (1523–6).

2. The word used by Sand for 'peasant uprising' is *jacquerie*, the earliest of which broke out in 1358.

3. The least well known of these is probably the artist Jacques Callot (*c.*1592–1635), whose most famous etchings depicted the miseries of war.

4. *The Vicar of Wakefield* (1766) is by Oliver Goldsmith (1728–74); *The Perverted Peasant* by Restif de la Bretonne (1734–1806); and *Dangerous Liaisons* by Pierre Choderlos de Laclos (1741–1803) – all eighteenth-century novels, the latter two of which show more cynicism than the first.

5. A quotation from Virgil's *Georgics* (III, 517–18).

6. 'Les Ormeaux' is French for The Elms.

7. Sand uses the traditional saints' days to refer to the two dates on which domestics would have been hired: St John's Day (24th June) in midsummer and St Martin's Day (11th November) in autumn.

8. Shepherdlass; one of Sand's Berrichon words (*pastoure*). Later on, Marie will tell Germain that he was never a shepherdlad (*pastour*).

9. A *galette* is a round flat cake.

10. Another local word, *brande*.

11. The word *livrée* (livery) often also referred to a ribbon given to the bride.

12. Two celebrated queens of England and France respectively, though Sand may have been thinking of Anne of Cleves rather than Anne Boleyn; the former was painted by Holbein, with a very elegant coif.

13. See Genesis 29 for the story of Jacob and Rachel.

14. The *exploit* was also often a branch decorated with a ribbon fixed to the bed of those invited to the wedding.

15. *Bazvalan* is a Breton word meaning a messenger of love.

George Sand was born Amandine-Aurore-Lucile Dupin in 1804. When she was four, her father died, and from then on Sand was brought up almost exclusively by her paternal grandmother in their native region of the Berry. In later life Sand would become an urbane, political figure, but her love for the Berry, its wildlife and people, never waned. Rural life was an important influence on her life and work.

When she was eighteen, Sand made a disastrous early marriage. Nine years later, she left her husband and moved to Paris, where she lived with her lover and early literary collaborator, Jules Sandeau. They wrote articles together and published a novel, *Rose et Blanche*, under the pen-name Jules Sand. In 1832, Sand brought out her first independent novel, *Indiana*, using the pseudonym G. Sand.

The novel was a great success, and henceforth Sand wrote with great fluency and speed. In her fiction, she criticised social conventions such as marriage and class society, and advocated passionate love – advice that she followed herself. Sand was politically, socially and literarily avant-garde – as well known for her androgynous dress sense and eminent lovers (Alfred de Musset, Frédéric Chopin) as for her written work. Her independence of spirit shocked nineteenth-century France.

During the 1840s, Sand became overtly political, founding the socialist *Revue indépendante*, and foregrounding the concerns of the working class in her fiction. But she also wrote books about the Berry which depicted the goodness of peasant life: a world untroubled by the Parisian political maelstrom. She was a keen literary experimenter – trying her hand at everything from political pamphlets to theatre. In 1854, she began to publish her monumental autobiography, *Histoire de ma vie*, and during the last decades of her life corresponded vigorously with other writers – including, most famously, her friend Gustave Flaubert. Sand's reputation as a rebel has helped to ensure that her pioneering and passionate writing has endured – and today, several of her novels are regarded as nineteenth-century French classics. She died in 1876.

Andrew Brown studied at the University of Cambridge, where he taught French for many years. He now works as a freelance teacher and translator. He is the author of *Roland Barthes: the Figures of Writing* (OUP, 1993), and his translations include *Memoirs of a Madman* by Gustave Flaubert, *For a Night of Love* by Emile Zola, *The Jinx* by Théophile Gautier, *Mademoiselle de Scudéri* by E.T.A. Hoffmann, *Theseus* by André Gide, *Incest* by Marquis de Sade, *The Ghost-seer* by Friedrich von Schiller, *Colonel Chabert* by Honoré de Balzac, *Memoirs of an Egotist* by Stendhal, *Butterball* by Guy de Maupassant and *With the Flow* by Joris-Karl Huysmans, all published by Hesperus Press.

HESPERUS PRESS CLASSICS

Hesperus Press, as suggested by the Latin motto, is committed to bringing near what is far – far both in space and time. Works written by the greatest authors, and unjustly neglected or simply little known in the English-speaking world, are made accessible through new translations and a completely fresh editorial approach. Through these classic works, the reader is introduced to the greatest writers from all times and all cultures.

For more information on Hesperus Press, please visit our website: **www.hesperuspress.com**

ET REMOTISSIMA PROPE

SELECTED TITLES FROM HESPERUS PRESS

Author	Title	Foreword writer
Pedro Antonio de Alarcón	The Three-Cornered Hat	
Louisa May Alcott	Behind a Mask	Doris Lessing
Edmondo de Amicis	Constantinople	Umberto Eco
Pietro Aretino	The School of Whoredom	Paul Bailey
Pietro Aretino	The Secret Life of Nuns	
Jane Austen	Lesley Castle	Zoë Heller
Jane Austen	Love and Friendship	Fay Weldon
Honoré de Balzac	Colonel Chabert	A.N. Wilson
Charles Baudelaire	On Wine and Hashish	Margaret Drabble
Aphra Behn	The Lover's Watch	
Giovanni Boccaccio	Life of Dante	A.N. Wilson
Charlotte Brontë	The Foundling	
Charlotte Brontë	The Green Dwarf	Libby Purves
Charlotte Brontë	The Spell	
Emily Brontë	Poems of Solitude	Helen Dunmore
Mikhail Bulgakov	Fatal Eggs	Doris Lessing
Mikhail Bulgakov	The Heart of a Dog	A.S. Byatt
Giacomo Casanova	The Duel	Tim Parks
Miguel de Cervantes	The Dialogue of the Dogs	Ben Okri
Geoffrey Chaucer	The Parliament of Birds	
Anton Chekhov	The Story of a Nobody	Louis de Bernières
Anton Chekhov	Three Years	William Fiennes
Wilkie Collins	The Frozen Deep	
Wilkie Collins	Who Killed Zebedee?	Martin Jarvis
Arthur Conan Doyle	The Mystery of Cloomber	
Arthur Conan Doyle	The Tragedy of the Korosko	Tony Robinson
William Congreve	Incognita	Peter Ackroyd
Joseph Conrad	Heart of Darkness	A.N. Wilson
Joseph Conrad	The Return	Colm Tóibín

Gabriele D'Annunzio	*The Book of the Virgins*	Tim Parks
Dante Alighieri	*The Divine Comedy: Inferno*	
Dante Alighieri	*New Life*	Louis de Bernières
Daniel Defoe	*The King of Pirates*	Peter Ackroyd
Marquis de Sade	*Incest*	Janet Street-Porter
Charles Dickens	*The Haunted House*	Peter Ackroyd
Charles Dickens	*A House to Let*	
Fyodor Dostoevsky	*The Double*	Jeremy Dyson
Fyodor Dostoevsky	*Poor People*	Charlotte Hobson
Alexandre Dumas	*One Thousand and One Ghosts*	
Joseph von Eichendorff	*Life of a Good-for-nothing*	
George Eliot	*Amos Barton*	Matthew Sweet
Henry Fielding	*Jonathan Wild the Great*	Peter Ackroyd
F. Scott Fitzgerald	*The Popular Girl*	Helen Dunmore
F. Scott Fitzgerald	*The Rich Boy*	John Updike
Gustave Flaubert	*Memoirs of a Madman*	Germaine Greer
E.M. Forster	*Arctic Summer*	Anita Desai
Ugo Foscolo	*Last Letters of Jacopo Ortis*	Valerio Massimo Manfredi
Giuseppe Garibaldi	*My Life*	Tim Parks
Elizabeth Gaskell	*Lois the Witch*	Jenny Uglow
Théophile Gautier	*The Jinx*	Gilbert Adair
André Gide	*Theseus*	
Johann Wolfgang von Goethe	*The Man of Fifty*	A.S. Byatt
Nikolai Gogol	*The Squabble*	Patrick McCabe
Thomas Hardy	*Fellow-Townsmen*	Emma Tennant
L.P. Hartley	*Simonetta Perkins*	Margaret Drabble
Nathaniel Hawthorne	*Rappaccini's Daughter*	Simon Schama
E.T.A. Hoffmann	*Mademoiselle de Scudéri*	Gilbert Adair
Victor Hugo	*The Last Day of a Condemned Man*	Libby Purves
Aldous Huxley	*After the Fireworks*	Fay Weldon

Alexander Pope	*Scriblerus*	Peter Ackroyd
Antoine-François Prévost	*Manon Lescaut*	Germaine Greer
Marcel Proust	*Pleasures and Days*	A.N. Wilson
Alexander Pushkin	*Dubrovsky*	Patrick Neate
Alexander Pushkin	*Ruslan and Lyudmila*	Colm Tóibín
François Rabelais	*Pantagruel*	Paul Bailey
François Rabelais	*Gargantua*	Paul Bailey
Christina Rossetti	*Commonplace*	Andrew Motion
Jean-Paul Sartre	*The Wall*	Justin Cartwright
Friedrich von Schiller	*The Ghost-seer*	Martin Jarvis
Mary Shelley	*Transformation*	
Percy Bysshe Shelley	*Zastrozzi*	Germaine Greer
Stendhal	*Memoirs of an Egotist*	Doris Lessing
Robert Louis Stevenson	*Dr Jekyll and Mr Hyde*	Helen Dunmore
Theodor Storm	*The Lake of the Bees*	Alan Sillitoe
Italo Svevo	*A Perfect Hoax*	Tim Parks
Jonathan Swift	*Directions to Servants*	Colm Tóibín
W.M. Thackeray	*Rebecca and Rowena*	Matthew Sweet
Leo Tolstoy	*The Death of Ivan Ilych*	
Leo Tolstoy	*Hadji Murat*	Colm Tóibín
Ivan Turgenev	*Faust*	Simon Callow
Mark Twain	*The Diary of Adam and Eve*	John Updike
Mark Twain	*Tom Sawyer, Detective*	
Giovanni Verga	*Life in the Country*	Paul Bailey
Jules Verne	*A Fantasy of Dr Ox*	Gilbert Adair
Edith Wharton	*The Touchstone*	Salley Vickers
Oscar Wilde	*The Portrait of Mr W.H.*	Peter Ackroyd
Virginia Woolf	*Carlyle's House and Other Sketches*	Doris Lessing
Virginia Woolf	*Monday or Tuesday*	Scarlett Thomas
Emile Zola	*For a Night of Love*	A.N. Wilson